BAD THINGS HAPPEN

BAD THINGS HAPPEN

KRIS BERTIN

BIBLIOASIS

WINDSOR ON

FIRST EDITION

Library and Archives Canada Cataloguing in Publication

Bertin, Kris, author
        Bad things happen / Kris Bertin.

Short stories.
Issued in print and electronic formats.
ISBN 978-1-77196-054-0 (paperback).--ISBN 978-1-77196-055-7 (ebook)

        I. Title.

PS8603.E76393B33 2016   C813'.6   C2015-907384-7
                                                 C2015-907385-5

Edited by Alexander MacLeod
Copy-edited by Emily Donaldson
Typeset by Chris Andrechek
Cover designed by Gordon Robertson

  **Canada Council for the Arts** **Conseil des Arts du Canada**   ONTARIO ARTS COUNCIL CONSEIL DES ARTS DE L'ONTARIO

 Canadian Heritage   Patrimoine canadien

Published with the generous assistance of the Canada Council for the Arts and the Ontario Arts Council. Biblioasis also acknowledges the support of the Government of Canada through the Canada Book Fund and the Government of Ontario through the Ontario Book Publishing Tax Credit.

PRINTED AND BOUND IN CANADA

Contents

This book is dedicated to my dear friends Alexander MacLeod and Ryan Paterson. Thank you both.

BAD THINGS HAPPEN

WHEN WE BROKE into his house, it was in the middle of the afternoon, so it felt like we weren't doing anything illegal. He had a stepladder leaned up against the side of his place, so it took nothing to get onto his little wooden balcony and through the sliding door.

All at once we'd done it. We were in hunky Jason Parvis's house. My heart was racing but we made an agreement beforehand that we would say nothing once we got in there, so I stayed quiet. The smell that hit us was overpowering. Like old gym socks and rotting milk. Garbage. Now that we were inside, we felt sick.

I didn't have a word for what it looked like. It wasn't just messy or dirty. It was crazy. The floors were clean, swept and mopped, but every surface was covered in stacks of stuff. Food wrappers from a year ago, receipts and old tissues and bills everywhere, protein shakes gone solid—at least ten of those. A coffee and side table piled with paper and plastic plates, brown with stains and crawling with flies. Tan pointed at a mouldy old cake in a plastic bubble sitting in the middle of the couch and made a gagging motion with her finger. I nodded, but I wasn't so much repulsed as worried. He was such

9

a normal-seeming guy, and so handsome and charming. I didn't know how a person could live like this, let alone imagine him doing it.

A weight bench with dirty laundry heaped over it. An old movie, broken in half with the tape torn out of it and hanging off the side of the dining-room chair. I'd picked up one half of it and read the title before putting it down. *Anal Hooker Hell*. There was a plastic jack-o-lantern hanging over the stairs, and when I saw it, I stood still, and stared. I counted all the months forwards and backwards from May and didn't know if it was from last Halloween or the next one coming. On the first three steps heading up there were three bowls. One was filled with broken glass, ash, and cigarette butts and the other two had more tissues, some apple cores, and plastic pens chewed into frayed blue sticks.

I said nothing, just shot glance after glance at Tan, but she didn't seem to notice. Too busy inspecting a pair of boxer shorts from the laundry weights, holding them up, looking closely for stains. Looking around, I had the feeling that everything had some deep meaning behind it, even if it didn't. Tan had found a giant Darth Vader bong on the table and was carrying it around with her, his underwear in her other hand. We had agreed not to touch anything, but I suddenly didn't want to stop her. If I could keep silent it would almost be like we'd never been here at all. I would just take what I'd learned and try to work with it as best I could.

Later, when it was over, we stayed silent for another five minutes, just walking up the road.

That was weird, I said.

Yeah, she agreed, looking at the sky. Fucked up.

And we might've gotten it out of our system if we'd bothered to talk about it, but instead Tan talked about her father. What he was like before he left. She'd never mentioned any of it before, and it seemed important not to interrupt her, but it felt like it had nothing to do with anything. Usually all she had to say was junk about her mother and how horrible she was. How she never wanted to end up like her, no matter what.

Jason was at the cash and we sort of didn't want to see him right away so we went in through the Carnation Food entrance instead of the Esso one. It was one of those half-and-half places with a gas station on one side and a restaurant on the other. We almost never went in the front because no matter what time of day it was you could smell grease and sausages and there were great big fat people and it all just grossed us out. Even if we wanted to get milkshakes or soup or whatever, we'd still go in through the side, then through the hallway between the store and the diner, where the bathrooms were.

But today we couldn't. It's not like Jason could even guess what we'd been up to but the both of us knew we couldn't talk to him yet. We were too wound up and I thought it made more sense to ease ourselves into it, so I led us in through the double doors, through the stinky egg smell and past the trucker hats and perms and sat where we never sat before.

What are you doing? Tan asked.

What?

We should act normal, she said.

I'm normal, I said. You're the one who's all skanked up.

And it was true, she was. She'd put on her sister's clothes and big earrings and a ton of makeup. Her

11

boobs were all jacked-up in a push-up bra but it wasn't sexy-looking. They just looked unnaturally swollen, like she was allergic to something. She'd been dressing like this a lot lately, but today it was like she'd gone above and beyond for our little B&E.

We should sit where we usually sit. Tan shook her head.

We usually sit over there so we can see *Jason*.

But it's weird to sit here. Even the waitresses think it's weird, look. Tan pointed over to the girls at the dairy bar, and they were looking at us, but probably only because she was pointing at them.

Don't point, I said. They already don't like us.

So? I don't like them either.

She flipped them the bird and they did the same right back.

I looked down. Carnation Food was the only place to work in Onecdaconis and in another year we'd be here with them, looking retarded in those hospital-green uniforms, smoking cigarettes and screwing up orders, calling people *hon*. Or at least I would be. Dad said I needed a job if he was going to get me a car like he did my brother, and I needed a car to do anything other than stand around at a gas station. To get the hell out of here.

What should I get? Tan was looking over the menu.

Just get whatever.

I just don't want to chunk out. I can feel it in my face the second after I eat something fatty. Tan squeezed her cheek. Especially if we're gonna go see *you-know-who*.

God Tanya, I rolled my eyes, don't call him that. Talk about suspicious. Listen to you.

Let's just stop talking about it, she said.

I agreed, and even went one further and stopped talking altogether.

Neither of us said anything, but it hung in the air between us. It was hanging there when Diane came over with a pot of coffee to take our orders, there when she had to come back a second and third time, and still there when she had to tell us if we weren't going to stop *fucking around* we had to leave. Over here's like, a place of business.

On the other side, Jason was leaning against the counter in his Esso polo shirt and track pants, chewing his nicotine gum. He looked so clean and healthy that for a minute it felt like we'd broken into the wrong house. My heart jumped a bit when I saw him, but it wasn't like I thought it would be. His smile cooled everything off, like even if he *did* know, he didn't care. It wasn't hard to act like things were normal.

When I said hi, it felt like always, but with Tan I could see something was different. She walked as if she were in heels on a runway even though she was in sneakers on linoleum.

Hey girls.

Jason, Tan said, like she barely noticed him. She wandered back to the magazines. He half-smiled at her, and looked to me for an explanation:

She got a date?

What? I laughed. Who would she be dating?

What's with the outfit, then?

I dunno. She didn't say.

Then her voice piped up from behind a GQ.

Are you talking about how I look, Jason?

You look great, Tan, he said flatly.

Then she moved her jaw around behind her lips, like when she's deciding whether to be mean or not. Instead, she asked him:

How old do you think I look?

I think you look like you're exactly sixteen, Tan.

I laughed, but when I looked over, Tan was red. She'd shut her magazine and was making a face at us.

I'm sorry, he said. I'm kidding.

She took a breath but that red was still creeping up her cheeks.

I bet I know how old you look today, Jason.

His wallet had been on his dresser in his filthy room. The two of us silently pulled it out of its leather slot, counted up the years on our fingers, just like I'd done with the pumpkin.

I immediately felt mortified to be next to him. I shot Tan a look, but she didn't notice.

You look thirty-four. Especially thirty-four today.

Yeah, he laughed, folding his big arms. What, did someone tell you how old I am?

You told us you were twenty-two, she spat. I wonder why you would do that?

Tan, I said sternly.

I never did that, he said.

Yes you did!

She shouted it, and shouted loud enough that everyone stopped moving or talking.

Then someone came in. We had to wait for him to pay for his gas and Tostitos and pick out an air freshener from the wall behind Jason before we could continue. He picked the orange one, Autumn Fresh. When he was gone Jason leaned over the counter and got serious. He said her name, but she ignored him.

Hey! He said, I'm talking to you, Tan.

She was spinning the rack of sunglasses, talking but not looking at him, another magazine under her arm.

I'm just saying. Why would a grown man need to lie about his age to a couple of girls? What would he *get* out of pretending to be closer to their age? Seems simple to me.

Jason came around from the counter to answer that one. I got smaller once he got near. We only ever talked to him from behind a row of gum and chocolate bars. He was huge, bigger than I thought he'd be.

If you're saying what I think you're saying, I might have to ask you to leave, Tan. Because people are already talking about me and the two little girls I let run wild back here, okay? So if you're gonna say that shit, you can leave right now.

Tan put on a pair of mirrored aviators before she faced him, and smacked her gum.

I'm not saying anything, she shrugged. I dunno.

She even put on a coy little smile before she turned around and tried another pair on.

Forget it, she said.

No, you'd better forget about it, Jason said. Then he deflated with a sigh and shook his head. I could see he was actually hurt now. Or maybe scared. He looked at the both of us and opened his arms.

I let you guys hang out here all day sometimes, I even let you have cigarettes *and* smoke them near the tanks. He shook his head again. You're my friends, but if you act like this, you won't be welcome here. Do you understand? This is really serious.

I held my breath.

Tan shot around and threw her magazine at him. And she screamed *loud*. Called him a stupid, lying faggot. Asshole-piece-of-shit. Words I'd never heard her use before, but that came out like she knew exactly how they were supposed to be used.

Tan! I shouted, but she was out the door, past the ICE freezer, past the parking lot and down the road. She stopped just once, and turned to see if I was coming after her. But the most I could give her was my voice, which had already bounced off the glass door and disappeared. I watched her walk down the hill towards the baseball diamond. In another minute, one of the managers from the restaurant popped her head in and Jason told her everything was fine. She was one of the moms that worked there, so she had to look at me before she was satisfied.

She's gone, I told the woman.

Finally, when her cheek lifted from the wall and she disappeared, he turned to me.

I don't mind if you guys hang out here, but *come on*. This is not fucking funny.

I'm not trying to mess anything up, Jason.

He took a deep breath and I stayed where I was.

We went out to the Baxter crates behind the store, where all the trash and cardboard got thrown. He was chewing his gum next to me, in the spot where Tan usually sat, while I smoked the cigarette she had given me. It was the first time he'd ever sat next to me, or come out here besides to tell us to make sure our butts were stamped out. I told him I had a question for him.

What? More allegations?

No. I looked at my shoes and cleared my throat. Nothing like that.

He looked at me.

Why are you here, Jason? I asked it quietly, like if I said it too loud he might know why I was asking.

What do you mean?

I mean Onecdaconis. You can go anywhere, why would you stay here?

He looked away:

It isn't so bad.

I just thought you were younger. I thought you were stuck here like us.

No. I don't know. I've lived other places and it's all pretty much the same.

Like where?

Like Vancouver or Montreal or whatever. He looked up at the trees hugging the property line, then motioned to my smoke.

Gimme that.

He took it from me and I watched him take a drag.

Seriously? Montreal's the same as here? I don't believe that.

It's people. He exhaled. People live everywhere you go, and everywhere you go, people are the same. There's just more or less of them.

He took a long drag, then another. By his third he offered it to me, but it was already almost gone. He coughed and cleared his throat.

I just prefer less, he said.

I sat with him, trying to make like what he was saying mattered to me, but all I wanted to know was how he ended up like this. What had gone wrong with his life, or if this was what life was always like.

How do you—

How do I what? He squeezed his eyes shut like it was sunny out, but it wasn't. For the first time, he really did look thirty-four.

Christ's sakes, Dee. What do you guys want from me? he asked. I didn't have an answer, but it wasn't like he was sticking around anyway. He put my cigarette out and went inside.

When we broke into his house, Tan was immediately drawn upstairs, into his bedroom, but I'd been more interested in the other rooms off the hallway. Downstairs was sort of tidied, or maybe arranged or something, but up here, everything was toppled over and cluttered. Two of the doors were blocked by boxes and old chairs and junk, but the third opened just the slightest bit. I made out a wardrobe with a mirror, small and red. Everything else was in boxes, everything except for a single umbrella with a bear on it hanging from the knob of the wardrobe. It was then that I realized there were no photos anywhere in the house. None of him or his mother or father or the family that might have been here at one time or another.

When I went back to Tan, I found her lying on the bed—his bed—smoking *his* cigarettes, sort of rolling back and forth. Her makeup was done—she must've done it in his little bathroom, the one filled with more clothes and junk and garbage, in the same mirror he shaved in. She twisted herself into a provocative pose, her blonde hair fanned out on the dirty pillows, smoking the cigarette like some kind of femme fatale. I watched her pout her red lips and produce perfect rings. These also felt like they meant something, even if they didn't.

Her mouth moved after that, and her eyes stared right at me, but nothing passed from her to me. The words stayed in her mouth instead. I motioned around us and mouthed back—about this place, about him, and about her, too—*what the fuck?*

And then, after a moment, after she shook her head like she didn't know, I mouthed something else. I did it with my head turned away because it was something just for me. Something my father would always say:

Who knows what's really going on at home.

It was later on that same week that I had to go looking for Tan. She didn't wake me up with the squirt bottle by my bed, didn't meet me on the trail by the river, and wasn't writing any dirty words in chalk along the highway. She wasn't at Carnation Food, or hanging around with Jason out front. Wasn't at the school, at the playground, at her Nan's. She wasn't anywhere, and when I called her mother, she was screaming so loudly into the phone I couldn't understand what she was saying.

After a few days, after her face and name had been put on flyers and broadcast on the radio, we'd learned she'd been seen getting into a truck with a pair of young men. Not at our truckstop, but at one over in Plaster Rock. I heard my parents talking about it downstairs, talking about what they would tell me.

At the same time I'd learned about Tan, I learned about Jason. That he'd had a family up at that house, years ago. It was a story I'd heard before, but hadn't meant anything to me because I didn't know who it was about. Because before this, it was like I was underwater—with Tan—while all the adult stuff went on above the surface. And now I had come up for air for the first time and could suddenly hear everything.

Jason's fiancée had left him because he was fucking around on her with some nineteen-year-old girl. Then he tried to commit suicide by driving off a bridge, except he fucked it up and someone managed to rescue him. Tan's sister told me all this, at the search-party meeting. All the different chairs in Tan's house had been taken from their spots at desks and the kitchen table and breakfast nook and the workroom in the garage, and put together in the living room, like we were having a makeshift wedding. Tan's sister was wearing a black dress and drinking wine, but everyone else was in hunter's orange and hiking boots, drinking tea or coffee or pop.

I ended up back at the Esso eventually. Jason was watching a car fill up, and I joined him across the counter, not knowing what else to do. I felt like I didn't have anyone else to see, or anywhere else to go. Right away, when I saw him, I knew I didn't like him anymore, and that I probably never had.

When he put his hand on me and asked how I was doing I told him that Tanya and I had broken into his house.

It's like some mental case lives up there, I said to him.

He cleared his throat and blinked and tried to say something.

After a moment, all he managed to say was bad things happen. It meant nothing to me, but he seemed to be satisfied with it, like that explained everything, his problems and Tan's problems and mine.

She didn't leave because of you, I said.

I think she did.

Well not in the way you think. She wanted to leave.

A bit later the police were there and had to talk to all of us. I told them the same thing—that she had wanted to leave. They wrote it down and moved on. Talked to everyone. Even questioned the ring of girls smoking in their green uniforms, no longer scowling at me, but instead stealing glances, like they didn't want to miss me falling to my knees or going into hysterics.

Instead, I waved at them. A few waved back. They were shivering and trying to keep their bare legs warm as the sun went down, and I realized I was doing the exact same thing.

MAKE YOUR MOVE

LET'S SAY YOU'RE a tough guy.

And by that I mean you're confident, self-assured. You don't take shit from people but you don't go around starting anything either. You don't have a code, or at least you wouldn't put it that way. You'd call it manners, but that wouldn't be it exactly. You'd call it minding your own business, but that isn't it either. Mostly you don't want to end up like the guys you know. Your father, doing twenty years in Dorchester. Your brother, all screwy on booze and schizophrenia drugs, walking around Barrington Street, yelling and in a panic and puffing his chest out like he owns the place.

Let's say you're in the bad part of town. You don't want to be, but you have to be because of your job. You're a driver, a limousine driver, but you're on foot. Another guy has your limo all day and at 11 p.m. you switch over and he gives it to you. Normally he comes to your house and then you drive to his, but tonight he says he's in trouble with his girl, and he doesn't have time to go all the way to your house. Normally you'd say too bad, come and get me if you don't want your lights punched out. But Alex has done right by you

23

lately, and he looked the other way when your unli-
censed cousin drove your shifts when you had the flu
so you could keep your sick days. So you say sure, and
you take the bus way uptown to the north end and
start walking with your fists all balled up, not wanting
to listen to your Walkman because you need all your
senses in these parts, your coat zipped up all the way so
that nobody sees your tie and thinks it means you have
money.

When you get to his house you have to wait, so you
lean on a fence surrounding his ten square feet of dead
grass. You'd like to have a cigarette but aren't sure if you
have enough time for one. There's nothing worse than
lighting one and having to save it for later.

So let's say you have your Player's Light anyway, and
it's good. You get a headrush because you only smoke
once in a while, but that makes you feel weak. Noodly
arms make you feel nervous, make you feel like you
can't fight, even though you can, even though you were
a top-tier middleweight on the circuit years ago (robbed
of the title because of judges' decision). Thinking about
this sours you, and when a couple of kids ask you for
smokes, you tell them to *take a walk*, and you even point
ahead to where they oughta go. Right away they start
with the name-calling, and the allegations are ludicrous:
that you're a cocksucker, that you suck your father's
pecker. You just stand there and take it, have a few more
puffs 'til they're done, and there's silence. That's when
you lunge at them.

You're careful not to actually hurt them, because you
like kids, but one of them doesn't react quickly enough
and his face bounces off your chest and you almost run
him over. The other one runs off in a straight line, as fast

as the other kid was slow, until he pops out of existence.

The slow kid gets a bloody nose and starts crying right there on the sidewalk. It reminds you of when your brother's friends busted *your* nose and laughed at you, left you in their front yard while they went to the store to snag some Whoppers and Twizzlers and whatever else. So let's say you take pity on the kid, and you take him with you in your limo, up front with you, behind the glass divider so that clients don't see him. After a while, you take him for a frosty at Wendy's and drive him home.

You meet his mother, Dawn, and she's a real knockout. You get the idea to tell her you saved the kid from a mugging, and he doesn't contradict you, but he doesn't go along with it either. It's three weeks later that he pipes up, because he's sick of you banging his mother five nights a week, but mostly because he hates having dinners with you, hates your boxing stories and your crude attempts at parenting him.

You and her break up and you walk home in the dark, in the rain, and you leave the city the next day, not because you're distraught but because this episode has signalled the need for a change, a clean break. You grow a moustache and get work bouncing at a bar that's straight all week and gay on the weekends. You get paid well but it's hard to find anybody who wants to be around you in this other city because the people are too modern and trendy for your sensibilities.

THE END

But let's say you don't light that smoke. You just twiddle your thumbs and wait for Alex, taking in the scenery. A couple kids walk by you, a bag lady stops and asks you for money and you don't give her anything because she actually looks like she could be working—you work, so why can't she? You don't tell her this, you don't say anything to her because people probably say that shit to her all the time, she's probably got a great comeback and you'd hate for her to get the upper hand on you. Alex comes and gives you the limo and on a whim you drive around with the divider down, something you almost never do.

A client named Lou appreciates the company and gives you a crisp $100 bill. His phone number is written on the money, but he doesn't strike you as a queer so you thank him and put it in your coat. It occurs to you that he looks more like an old-school gangster, real calm and cool with one of those haircuts that's slicked back so severely it's pulling his face upwards. You wonder if the number is an opportunity to become some kind of mob goon. Maybe he liked the look of you— you have a kind of pompadour, not quite like his, but close—like at least you're on the same page hair-wise. Maybe he liked your boxing stories, that line about how winning isn't *winning*, just like the law ain't *the law*, if he knows-what-you-mean.

After you drop him off you hit Wendy's for a frosty. The teens working there really dig a limo coming through the drive-thru, and for some reason you get the urge to pay with the big bill, to really knock their socks off.

Let's say you don't break the $100 bill though, because you want the number on it. You just pay with pocket change but you leave a five-dollar tip because those kids work damn hard and the girl in the window is cute enough. She looks a bit like your aunt, the one that always made you feel weird, made you blush when she'd kiss you or make prolonged eye contact. You try to put her out of your mind, but the frosty is right there in the cup-holder, reminding you of her all night and you end up squirming around in your seat with a big erection for the rest of your shift. When you finally get rid of it the next morning your brain starts working again and you remember the number on the bill and decide to call it.

. A lady picks up and you say that this number was written on one of your bills. She says she's glad you called and tells you to come see her tonight. Turns out you got it all wrong, she wrote *her* number on Lou's bill, and you ended up with it by mistake. But you like the sound of her voice so you ask where you should come see her and she says *the bar, stupid. Ron's. And it's Loretta, in case you already forgot.*

You say *how could I forget* because you're feeling desperate and aren't sure if you can go another month without being touched by another person.

You go there before work and hold up the money until someone comes over and you ask if she's Loretta. She says no, she's Dawn, but she's so beautiful you don't even care about Loretta anymore. You ask for a club soda because you've been clean for eight months now and while she's gone you get your Maritime Limo pen and cross out Loretta's number and put yours on it because it's actually a pretty cool thing to do. She seems annoyed that you're paying for a one-dollar drink with a hundred-dollar bill, but you leave her twenty bucks on top of that and start bothering her about dating you. She gives up or gives in, partially because of your charms, partially because she's drawn to thuggish kinds of guys, partially because you're genuinely interested in her.

You have your first date that night, sort of. She drives around with you with the divider up, and you talk all night about the city, about where you grew up, about your hopes and dreams. Dawn's nervous but excited, sometimes talks too fast, sometimes not at all. In the morning, you have to take the limo to Alex's and it turns out she lives nearby, right around the corner. Instead of going home, she invites you in, and you sleep together—actually sleep because you're so tired.

It's when you wake up that you fuck, and it's so nice you tell her you love her by accident. It's a thing you do sometimes when you're having sex, sometimes when you're being served food; once you said it to your corner when a big Newfoundlander gave you one right on the jaw and you went down.

When you see Dawn next, you and her and her son go for a day-trip to the beach out by the campgrounds and you ask her to marry you then and there. But you ask so quietly and it's so windy and the gulls keep screaming so loud that she doesn't hear you. You think she's ignoring you and you're so embarrassed you don't even stay for the sandwiches she packed. You don't return her calls and you never see her again, though you go to that beach to think about your life whenever you're feeling blue. You throw rocks at the birds. You write shit in the sand. Sometimes you swim, sometimes you don't.

THE END

Let's say, though, that you don't hang onto that hundred-dollar bill. You get caught up in the moment and want to be a big shot, so you give it to the drive-thru girl who looks like your aunt, slip the money to her like it's no big deal. You don't really think it through, and you momentarily forget that you're the guy driving the limo, not the guy in the back of it, not the guy with money and class and complimentary champagne. The look she gives you is so sexy that something misfires in your brain and you forget that you need this money, you really do, and instead you say *keep the change.*

She asks if you're serious, and for a moment you nearly tell her you aren't, you nearly grab it from her hand and tear out of there, but you don't. You just keep your mouth shut and give her a look like it *ain't no thing*, not to a guy like you. You're caught off guard when she tells you she's off in fifteen minutes, and her and some friends are going camping and do you want to come?

You really shouldn't, you need this job, and you'll get fired for sure, but the kind of mood you're in, you say fuck it. You won't just come, you'll do her one better and *drive* her there.

Before long, her and six other kids in Wendy's uniforms are in the back with towels and coolers full of snacks, bopping around a beach ball and drinking beers. You turn off your radio and just go with the flow, burn up company gas until you get to the campgrounds, and start drinking with the kids, drinking as fast and as hard as you can so that awkwardness, that divide between your age and theirs, can't be felt. Actually, most of them are college-aged, but it's little Jessie, the one who looks like your aunt who's the youngest, over fifteen years younger than you. Despite your best efforts you start feeling the years after you make reference to Midnight Express and she doesn't know what you're talking about.

You get a horrible feeling in the pit of your stomach and you wonder if there's some way you can come up with an excuse for the three-and-a-half hours you just threw away acting like an idiot. Someone passes you a joint and you take a deep hoot, then a few more even though you shouldn't—you've had a fifty-fifty chance of a bad trip with the stuff since high school, and it did nothing but damage to your brother. Still, it takes the edge off and you're able to just chill out and make your move.

Jessie and you are on a picnic table on the beach, alone, away from the all the others, when she starts talking about her sister, a single mother with a son from a deadbeat dad. A real piece of shit that used to slap her around. You want to say big deal, you were slapped around, and your mother was too, and her mother before that, and there are worse fucking things than that all around us. You don't say this, and instead you say fuck it and start kissing her, and she's into it, making little sounds like she's in heaven. She starts moving her body around in a weird little dance and it seems like this is so easy it's not even interesting anymore.

But let's say you stay the night. You go back to her tent. The sex isn't very good, and after she says it was amazing even though time seemed to slow down and you had real bad cottonmouth and kept smacking your tongue when you were on top of her.

You and her join the rest of her friends around the camp-fire and one of the guys is playing the guitar, singing Oasis songs while another guy plays one of those stupid little bongos that fits in your lap, and he can't keep the beat whatsoever. You take it from him and start doing it. They start laughing, half because you're so good at it, half because you're the limo driver they met at the drive-thru, now out here with your pants rolled up, a blanket around your shoulders with your tie still on. They're laughing but you don't care, you're so into it that you're on fire. You tell them it's because you used to box, you got rhythm, you got skills.

You start telling them about your fight with Johnny-Cakes Turner, where you cleaned his clock because of your footwork alone. Rhythm. Halfway through your story, something catches your eye in the background, and you swear, you *swear* it's a ghost. A chubby, glowing one, just like in the Ghostbusters movie. It's going back and forth from the picnic table and the treeline again and again and it's so fucked up you say *oh my god* as many times and in as many ways as you're able to before you trip and fall forward and begin a whole new kind of existence on your hands and knees.

THE END

Let's say, on the other hand, that you don't stay with Jessie. You tell her you gotta take a dump and ask where the toilets are. You make a break for your limo through the darkness, your shoes crunching on the gravel path, a chill going through you.

One of the kids catches you getting behind the wheel and says you can't drive. You tell him you're just going to get some chips at the canteen. He tells you you're drunk and they already have lots of chips, plus there is no canteen. But he's trying to do you a favour, trying to keep you from getting a DUI or smashing up your limo. He isn't aware you're trying to strand them all out here, roll onto the highway and never come back, so when he opens the door to get the keys away, he's being gentle, almost brotherly about the whole thing.

He is totally unprepared for the way you twist his wrist all up and start driving with the door open. He

31

makes this sound somewhere between laughter and screams because he doesn't know you well enough to know if you're kidding. Once you start driving, *really driving*, and he has to run to keep up, he realizes you aren't kidding. That you're willing to take this all the way up from misdemeanor to felony, and that he has to do something before you get there. He tries to get a hold of the wheel and for a minute he almost does before you punch him in the back of the head so that he just disappears into the dark.

Hours later you're sobering up at an all-night diner, and between sips of black coffee you notice in the shining silver napkin holder that the kid scratched your face bad, three diagonal lines right across your cheek like someone attacked you with a camping spork. Suddenly you're inspired—you realize you could call into work and say that you were carjacked, but you got the limo back. You could even make like you *took care* of the jacker—not actually say it, but kind of imply it. You hold the napkin holder up and have a good look at yourself. Would it be a believable story?

You decide that yeah, if some piece-of-shit-minority guy tried to steal your ride, that's exactly what you'd do. He'd be in your trunk right now, bound and gagged, all his facebones broken. You start drawing pictures of the imaginary man's face on a stack of napkins, start to practice how you're going to tell the story. Three more refills and a whole breakfast plate later, you've basically drawn a thirty-panel comic book about it, six-napkins long.

When you call your boss and launch into your performance, you use your little pictures like flashcards, and it really works. You aren't sure if it works because you're a good actor (though back in high school, Mrs. DePalma from English 3 said you could've been an actor), or because of the reputation of guys like your brother and your father, or because your boss is just an idiot.

He gives you the rest of the night off, but you say no, you'll work, and so you're off to your next job, sent back to the hotel, back to get Lou, who asked for you specifically. You take him to a bar called Ron's and he comes back with two ladies, two waitresses, Loretta and Dawn. He introduces you as the Champ and tells them the story you told him, except it's all ass-backwards and he gets every name wrong, but you don't correct him. Turns out Lou isn't a gangster, he owns a car lot somewhere in Clayton Park, sells Chevy trucks and Jeeps. At some point he sends Dawn to sit up front with you, probably because he's going to get blown.

You don't talk because you're already getting a hangover, and she doesn't talk because she doesn't like the look and probably the smell of you.

You realize that the longer you go without talking the scarier you probably seem, and the more menacing your injured face looks. When you offer her a cigarette, she jumps in her seat, then says no, then asks if she can go home. You take her there and it turns out to be practically next door to Alex. She leaves without saying goodbye to you, though she telephones Lou and Loretta with the direct line and says a secret into the receiver.

A month later you're at a pet shop buying tropical fish food and maybe a few more fish, maybe another clownfish, because yours haven't been looking very fresh lately. You're looking at their selection, walking around in a Hawaiian shirt (because it's laundry day and the only other clean shirt has your own face on it from your fighting days and you're not going to wear that in public) when you run into her and a young boy holding a stick with a ball tied to the end.

She doesn't recognize you, but you recognize her, and when you say hello she doesn't respond so you pretend to inspect ceramic aquarium decorations like it never happened. She walks by you and out of your life forever, but you realize the ceramic castles are actually pretty neat. There are eight different kinds of castles, eight different colours, eight different ways to go, so you buy them all and are happy with your purchase.

At home you arrange them like they're warring kingdoms on your coffee table and when you lean in and squint really hard, you can just barely see peasants walking around on the cobblestones, little people with their whole lives ahead of them.

THE END

THE NARROW PASSAGE

GENE AND RICHARD saw the smoke before they saw the people. Billowing up into the air and lit by the dull glow from a fire, it looked like a thick, orange neck and head sticking out of the treetops. It was early in the morning— before the sun had risen, when the sky was the darkest blue it could be without being called black—and the fire was the only source of light. Richard couldn't think of anything other than a burning house to explain it, didn't imagine anyone would be up at this hour if something hadn't gone wrong. He thought he would see people standing outside a home falling in on itself, burping out sparks and smoke and flames. He thought they would be weeping, and clutching each other, watching everything come apart. He wanted to say something about it, but Gene—who had talked all morning long—was silent.

Then, once they passed through a clearing and went over a bridge made of logs and planks that sat in a pool of stagnant water, he saw them. Maybe fourteen of them—men and women—in lawn chairs, sitting inside a circle of four-wheelers and pickup trucks, surrounding a blaze wide enough to throw a body into. They were drinking, and smoking. Richard could smell weed.

All of them raised their bottles to Richard and Gene when they got out of the truck. Dogs were barking.

One of the men turned towards them and called:

How ya doing?

He was Gene's age, bald and bearded and with a roll of fat around his head and neck like a lion's mane. He had a big black dog by the collar, pulling it up and off the ground while it croaked out its barks. Gene didn't answer him, but Richard did, without looking at them:

Not too bad, how are you?

He looked at the plot of land, lit by the truck's headlights. It was lumpy and uneven without a single blade of grass present and there were three different houses up on posts, their foundations gone or not yet poured. There was every kind of dogshit scattered about, from fresh and brown to hard and black, all the way to the dry stuff, white like powdered donuts. The main house in the middle had a pitched roof and a fence made of pulpy birch logs, front steps leading to a sinking porch. A cold room filled right to the ceiling with debris that Richard couldn't make out. Things in bags—maybe cans and plastic containers—and stacks of what might be firewood. The bonfire was off to the side of one of the houses, a few feet away from a flap of construction plastic where a wall should have been.

There was a piece of metal nailed to the porch that looked like the back of a license plate, hand-painted with thick, orange paint:

The Cliftons.

Richard and Gene had been going for a long time already, collecting garbage since 4 a.m. Their truck was a modified cube truck with the top peeled off like a sardine lid, and it was full. The two-by-fours that hinged across the back—gates that were always wet with garbage juice and dark with grime, and which could be closed, one by one, as the garbage pile grew in the back—looked ready to pop. This load was a big one, and though they were outfitted with a hydraulic for dumping, there was none for crushing like the trucks from the city had, so there wasn't much they could do about it.

It was only when Richard finally took his eyes away from the place that he saw what they had left for them. Instead of garbage cans, there were seven rusted drums that were deep and without any kind of lid. Gene was already working on it. He was bent over, pulling at a bag that had taken on rainwater and was suctioned to the inside of the barrel. There were a dozen more bags thrown nearby, sitting in the dirt. One—which was the furthest from the cans and seemed to have been thrown from one of the houses—was burst. They were supposed to accept no more than five per household. Even if they treated this place as three houses, they had exceeded their limit just with the bags left on the ground.

But Gene said nothing, so Richard went to work alongside him. It was his first week and he was being careful.

After wrenching soaking-wet bags that weighed up to twenty pounds from their barrels, they had to throw them—overhand, maybe fifteen feet up—over the gates and into the heap. A few fell off and Richard had to catch up with them, throw them back up.

When he heard laughter, he took another look at the bodies around the fire and tried to guess if they were laughing at him and Gene. He decided it didn't matter. They were big people, overweight and bearded, wearing down-filled vests, boots. Some of them were young, too young to be there. Two boys with long, bare necks sticking out of hooded sweatshirts, watching him closely. There was a girl with a long yellow braid of hair hung over an open parka, her skin chalky white like she was kept indoors except for special occasions like this. She was maybe twelve. One of the bigger men was fanning the flames with an enormous cedar bough and she was laughing.

Just from the amount of embers in the bonfire and the size of the brush pile beside it, Richard guessed that the fire had been burning for twelve hours. Standing upright by the blaze was a grandfather clock. At first he'd thought it was a person. Out of the corner of his eye, he watched it tilt, then rise and glide towards them in the dark. Someone was walking it to them.

Got room in there still? They called.

It was already before them when Gene said *yes, go ahead.*

Three of them came to the truck—one of the boys and two of the men. A fourth, an old man wearing a mustard-coloured coat too big for him, came to supervise. He looked frail and weak, his face full of lines like a mud puddle sucked dry by the sun.

Thank you boys, he said.

No problem, Gene replied.

The men stumbled against the truck and the young one climbed the back gate, guided the clock upwards with one hand while the two men lifted. Richard and Gene backed up and watched the clock float up to the top of their truck before disappearing into the black-and-green heap.

The old man touched Richard above the elbow and he was surprised to feel strength in his grip. And his hand was burning hot, hot enough to radiate through the fabric of Richard's jumpsuit. He said:

Thank you so very much.

His eyes were burning too.

Gene was quick to answer, and repeat himself:

No problem here.

Nothing stayed hidden.

Once a bag went from the truck to the sorting-centre floor and up into the hopper, it would be torn open by a row of men in thick, padded gloves. They saw everything: mould of every colour, adult diapers, stinking turkey carcasses and newspapers, abandoned photo albums and entire outfits—shoes and hats and pressed suits—as if a person had been dissolved in the garbage bag and only their outermost layer remained.

And then there was the stranger stuff, what they didn't expect to see. Items that peeked out from cantaloupe guts and coffee grinds and used tissues. The realness of a man's blonde toupee, wet and gleaming from the contents of a nearby plastic bottle of chicken stock. An old scarecrow made of pantyhose and chicken wire, twisted up like a circus rubberman. A hundred or so tiny ceramic busts of Mozart, all identical, most of them still intact and smiling painted smiles. Dozens and dozens of smudged brass casings from spent ammunition all mixed in with heaping strings of red-and-brown animal entrails. Three deer heads, stinking and staring and missing an oval of skull where there had once been antlers.

It wasn't their job to stop and watch the sorters descend on their load, but nearly every one of the rural guys—the guys who didn't work for a company—they always stayed and watched it feeding in. Gene would walk right up to them, join the sorters and stare at the bags he'd previously made guesses about. The ones that were overly heavy or strangely shaped. He'd even reach in and poke at things, smiling, a cigarette hanging from his mouth.

On his first day, when Richard asked why they were waiting around, Gene had frowned:

I've been doing this since before there even was a sorting centre, he said. Since before you were even born.

Richard felt a quick burst of anger in his chest, but was careful to keep it inside him. He needed this job. When Gene hired him—when Richard walked the three miles along the highway to get to his house—he made it clear he had no problem getting rid of him. He said it while they drank instant coffees, sitting at a tiny vinyl table in the garage.

First, he listened to Richard's story about buying a trailer with his wife, away from town, and how he'd been laid off from his roofing job. About how seasonal work had just ended and that he'd spotted Gene's ad on the bulletin board at the Co-op. A story that was mostly true, one that left out an argument over pay with the roofers, and something similar at an apple orchard weeks before that.

Richard had been careful to make himself seem strong and useful, and not too needy, even though he was that as much as the first two. He could feel himself split in three, between the person he was, the one he claimed to be, and the one he wanted to become.

It had worked and Gene had shook his hand, saying *the job's yours* before he set Richard straight:

I don't need to be doing any favours to anyone, he said. If you can't keep up or do it right or listen to me, I can find another fella as quick as I found you.

Of course, Richard said.

So at the sorting centre Richard just stood back and let Gene have his fun. He liked to show off the *what-the-fucks* but also the *perfectly goods*. A pressed shirt in its crinkly plastic package, still sealed, still with that bit of cardboard around the collar, a price tag. A Con-Air hair-dryer, still in its box, boasting *Salon Performance*. Two-dozen fresh cabbages, immaculate and waxy green like they'd been bought that day, spinning away like model planets down the conveyer belt.

He could explain their origins too. The box of Pal-O-Mine chocolate bars still in shrink-wrap came from a household of compulsive eaters who were trying to turn things around. A giant freezer bag full of pill bottles and loose tablets and powder mixes were uppers that probably belonged to the DeLongs, who were husband and wife—and both truckers—and needed this sort of thing to get through their lives. He connected a cheap police-man's costume to the Tremblay boy, a senior in high school—who might have started the highway tire fire in October wearing this very costume—who was trying out for the RCMP next year.

He'd start the same way, by saying *what this is here*, and then gave Richard something that it had him taken years to understand. A map he'd made in his mind, that he could unfold and lay out and point to at a moment's notice, with pride. Richard understood that this was why they were here. Gene was proud of what he knew, but presented it as basic information that Richard needed in order to do the job. Something he'd share, quietly, respectfully, but as a simple fact, the same way he'd show how to work around the sticky part of the clutch, or the best place to tip their load once they pulled into the sorting centre.

Richard imagined that Gene had been in this place so long that the facts had simply stuck to him. He had grown up in town, in apartments, and moved a lot, and felt like he never learned anything. He had a neighbour who fought with his wife, but he'd only ever heard any of it when he was exactly on the other side of the wall from them. With Gene, it was as if he had been listening outside of every house, all the time—and all at once—for as long as he'd been alive. It felt like he had access to every river, every stream flowing beneath the surface of all the houses, all the lives on their route. He could pan out the hard little nuggets that told a story about the world above.

To Richard, this was a waste of time. All of it was equal. All of it was garbage and deserved to get down the chute with the eggshells and the willow branches and the phonebooks and all the plastic and paper rattling away on the belt. All of it—everything that was separate—would come together and become a single torrent, gushing into the system.

When Gene sorted through their load, Richard couldn't stand to take part. He would stare out the hangar doors and watch it all emptying out in the landfill, watch the seagulls picking through it. Stared at the spot where it collected and joined slow-moving waves of pulp and debris, mounting and tumbling over as the bulldozers ploughed through the grey tide.

There were four legs to the garbage run. Routes that Gene had been driving and collecting from for more than three decades.

The first leg was all the houses strung along the main road, all in a line. These houses were mostly well built, if not large, and had garages, sometimes boats. Big lawns, front and back, edged by the forest. This was where Gene lived. Everyone knew him and would wave to him. Some left notes for him, taped to their cans.

Gene,

Sorry about the extra junk, Jill went off to college this week and we had a big clean up. Back to three bags next week (or less) we can promise you that!

Thank you,

Mike & Louise

The second leg was made of all the cul-de-sacs that had sprung up in the last twenty years, houses that were all pretty much identical. Almost all of them two storeys with white siding and black-shingled roofs. Almost all of them inhabited by military families who didn't want to live on the base. Producers of very little trash, except for cardboard boxes from all the shuffling they did across the country. Always in a pile, always tied with twine and set in the very corner of the lawn, beside a pair of cans. If nobody gave them too much, if the weather was good, and their truck was in good health, the first two runs could sometimes be done in one day.

The fourth leg was the Pine Crest Trailer Park, where Richard and his wife lived. Gene explained that they did it last because it had lots of stops and could take a long time, though it was generally a lesser load for the simple fact that the households were so small. One time, Richard picked out a single grocery bag filled with paper plates and hotdog packages, crushed drink boxes

43

and chip bags that represented the total waste from a single trailer. Richard held it up like a prize and threw it in effortlessly, like a ball of paper into a wastebasket.

Thank god for the deadbeat dads, Gene said to Richard once they were back in the truck. Richard laughed because he felt he was supposed to.

The third leg of the run was the rural route.

This was a place Richard had never seen before. Even when he was in junior softball, and he and his mother had to drive out to places like Tracy and Lincoln and Clayton and Maugerville, he had never gone down those roads. Gene said it was a place that was in between places, too far out to be collected by any other contractor but him. He explained that it wasn't really part of the county's responsibility, but it had somehow been lumped into their route by someone in the seventies. Explained it like it was an embarrassing thing that had happened to him personally.

We're following the river, because that's how all the settlers got here. Back then you couldn't go through hills and rock, you had to go around, Gene said. That's why the road's shit. Everyone moved away and forgot about it.

The other places had their names posted on signs that were put up by someone who cared, who had one made with municipal funds, either by a machine or a draftsman with a paintbrush and a sense of design. They said:

WELCOME TO STOCK

and

The Village of Kennedy

and

You are entering
the community of
LONG LAKE

But on the third leg nothing was written. There was just the moment when you were on pavement, surrounded by trees, and the moment after when the road turned to dirt or mud where swamp crept across ditches. Their truck did well enough on the rest of their route, but here it shook and shuddered and groaned from overwork. When their shocks started to shriek, Richard knew they had passed over. The place was called the narrows, or sometimes Kennedy Narrows, or the old township. Richard had heard Gene use all three, and once heard an old man at the diner call it *the narrow passage*.

Heading up the narrow passage today?

Not today, Gene said. Thank the lord.

It took a half hour of driving down a logging road just to get to the first house, which was nothing more than a wooden shack next to an old gas station canopy with no gas station in sight. A pile of wood, a towtruck and a lot of cars parked where the pumps must have been. Once, they saw an old woman asleep in the towtruck, and another time they saw her in a lawn chair with a blanket pulled up over her.

Out there the workload doubled, even though there were fewer houses than even the first leg. Where it sometimes took five minutes of driving to get to the next house, and where Richard and Gene uncovered cans and found far more than they were supposed to even take. The limits, which kept them from having to dump at the sorting centre several times a day, and which would have been useful here, went ignored. In any of the other three legs of the run, if someone left too much, Gene would march up to the door, and knock—even in the dark of early morning—to set them straight. But in the old township, he did no such thing. Here, all the rules were different—bent and reshaped, or even ignored—and Gene was quiet about this inconsistency.

The first time Richard was able to address it, after eight months of working with Gene, he did it carefully. They had just pulled thirteen bags from a rotting wooden bin that had pushed itself apart from the weight. He didn't look at Gene's face, staring ahead, instead, at the sinking little trailer where it came from. He asked:

Do you want me to talk to them?

He had learned by then not to ever make any kind of accusation against Gene. He could only make a suggestion about himself, and what he could do for his boss.

Gene responded by shaking his head without looking at him:

They've been here longer than I have. Were here before we even had the rules.

Later he added, at the sorting centre that—to be fair—a lot more people lived out here than on the rest of the run. Even if there were fewer houses, there were more people inside of them.

Then, because he was away from it, and in a place he felt comfortable, he added:

It's different out there.

Houses were bungalows and saltboxes, sometimes with garages, but usually not. Some had house numbers, but others didn't. A string of newer-looking mini-homes had their civic numbers spray-painted on boulders at the edge of the properties. There were a few active farms, seated in rolling hills, but plenty more stretches of farmland where families lived and did no farming. Where fences surrounded empty corrals, and chicken coops made of greying wood leaned in on themselves, ready to collapse.

Early on, Richard asked him where the animals were, and Gene told him there had never been animals out here as long as he remembered. The only ones they saw were wild, deer or moose. Once, they saw a black bear saunter out of the open doorway of an old church that Gene said had once been the school, too.

About this place, Gene had no theories to share, and at the sorting centre had none of his usual vigilance with the third leg's load. He waited and watched, shyly and silently, off to the side. Suddenly his duties seemed ceremonial, his attendance merely compulsory.

Another time, they came across four plastic barrels at a curb, too heavy to lift, stinking and sloshing with some kind of liquid. When they took the lid off and saw a putrid black substance that Richard knew could only be the contents of a dredged septic tank, Gene said *for fuck's sake.*

Then he put the lid back on and walked away from it.

We have to report this, Richard said. Don't we? This is hazardous material, right?

Leave it, Gene said.

Later, when they were back in the truck, Gene explained as best he could:

I didn't grow up out here. I don't know why it's like this.

The Clifton farm, Richard noticed, was always in flux.

Sometimes the yard would be overrun with things, with La-Z-Boy chairs and dressers and desks, swollen from rainwater or separating into thick layers like roast-beef sandwiches. Little broken pieces everywhere and stacks of cardboard boxes gone hairy with mould and plastic bags blowing around like tumbleweeds. Other times, like in the summer, it would be bare, picked clean, and almost normal-looking. Just an ordinary property that was on its way to becoming somewhere you'd want to live. Then, it could be overrun with junk cars like Sunfires and Tercels and more half-ton trucks and four-wheelers parked crookedly on the dirt lawn.

That's when there would be beer bottles and forty-ouncers left standing upright in the ground, or lying where they had come to rest after rolling away from a sweaty hand. Or on the road, shattered into brown necks and bottoms from their trip through the air and across the dead earth.

The things that they'd spotted on the lawn sometimes ended up at the curb, a week later, and items that they had passed over at other curbs sometimes ended up on the Clifton lawn too. And even though Gene had named the very things they picked up and threw into the truck as *unhaulable* everywhere else, Richard knew better than to make anything of it. From the Cliftons, they would take mattresses and boxsprings, a beer fridge and a deep freeze, a ride-on lawnmower with its wheels and seat and steering wheel dismembered.

After the bonfire, Richard didn't see any of the people who lived there for a long time.

It was rare to even see anyone awake during the earliest part of the run anyway, except for the farmers who'd wave from their tractors on the third leg, or the army guys running with weighted packs on the second leg who wouldn't. Sometimes they saw young men in camouflage jackets on four-wheelers with rifles, buzzing alongside the truck in the ditches. But Gene and Richard were both always on the look-out for a Clifton.

When Richard finally saw one of them again, it was winter. Two of the women, both of them large with long, blonde hair, getting little Cliftons in snowsuits down the steps of the main house and into the van. Later, they'd seen the old man carrying what looked like two bottles of Javex from one house to another, early in the morning, wearing a short jacket over a robe and rubber boots. The old man stopped. His hands were full, so he didn't wave, but he nodded at them.

Good morning boys, he called.

That was the day before Gene finally explained about them, rotating his neck carefully before he spoke, making sure it was in the right place. They were in the truck.

Their brains are scrambled, Gene said quietly.

A gentle explanation, long overdue. A guilty look on his face.

That's what I figured, Richard said. Crazy people.

Then Gene leaned in, his hand nearly touching Richard's.

They've hurt people, he said. More than a few.

Really?

Two of them did, he said. The brothers. Or cousins. It was a long time ago but everyone remembers it.

Richard didn't know what Gene wanted him to say, so he said nothing. They were on the fourth leg, the furthest they could be from the third. Before the silence went for too long, Richard tried a joke:

They didn't shoot their garbage men, did they?

Richard smiled, and waited for one in return. Gene's moustache widened for a moment, but no teeth flashed from underneath. His mouth became small and said *ha*.

After months, the work hadn't gotten easier. With Gene, there were no easy days.

Richard had worked past the pain, like he figured Gene must have, but he almost couldn't cope with the smell. It stayed with him even after he changed and cleaned, even though his wife said she could smell nothing on him. He learned it was something that was still inside him when he made a tiny cone out of toilet paper to scour the insides of his nostrils with. He understood that he was taking it home with himself, in little pieces, particles that were hiding wherever they could. Something that was so dangerous to him that his body set off alarms at the presence of even the tiniest bit of it. Deadly harmful, but ordinary and ever-present, sitting in every single driveway, produced by mere existence; which grew, and would continue to grow and thrive so long as there were people to keep feeding it. When he cleaned himself, Richard imagined that whatever specks he washed off would look like the landfill in miniature, that up close it would look like the same writhing, grey heap, clinging to him.

The job was only four days of work, but each day could drag on for twelve to fourteen hours. Other than trips to the dump, and when they would pull over to piss, Gene gave them one lunch break, and took Richard to the same diner off the highway every shift.It was in the next county, but nearest the sorting centre, so they could eat having already dumped their first load. They would order first, then go to the bathroom together, unzip their coveralls to the waist, and soap their arms up past their elbows. Set the taps as hot as they could stand and wash until the water in the sink was clear and their skin was red.

You wash good or you get sick, Gene said. The only people who clean better than us are surgeons.

Then, with their elbows lifted and their hands forward, they'd return to their table and eat as much as they could stand to put inside their bodies. This was also something that Gene instructed Richard to do on his first day, something that Richard failed to do. It was noon but they had already been going for seven hours.

We're going until it's dark out so eat up.

Richard ate most of a plate of fish and chips and had a cup of coffee. Didn't really touch his peas. And then he watched Gene eat a hamburger and fries, a bowl of tomato soup that came with a roll, a big chicken Caesar salad swimming in dressing and bacon bits, and a cinnamon bun. He ate by opening his mouth and pushing the food in, letting his throat and jaws work on their own. He didn't try to speak, or even look around. He was focused entirely on the next bite and nothing else. He drank a coffee and a water and an orange juice in big gulps between mouthfuls and finished the coleslaw on Richard's plate before he was done.

Four hours later, Richard found himself falling behind Gene. He began to miss his throws into the truck, going through the motion of it without looking. Another time he failed to pay attention to the weight and integrity of a bag, covered himself in wood ash and cat litter when it all came apart at the apex of his throw.

And Gene kept going.

He was sixty-one with grey cheeks and a moustache, had a stomach that protruded from under his coveralls, bad knees and bursitis in his elbow. He had difficulty turning his neck and said it could get locked into place if he wasn't careful. And he could move faster, more efficiently than Richard, who was thirty-six and thin, who had once been on the football and rugby team and who played softball in an amateur league for a decade. On the last half of the first day, Gene was emptying cans and throwing three bags for every one of Richard's. He had done it for long enough that he knew exactly how much of himself to put into every movement. Took all of his available energy and divided it evenly between households, filled himself up with the exact amount of calories needed to do it all over again.

On his first day, in the time it took Richard to retrieve a bag that had gotten away from him, he saw Gene climb the gates of the truck and get on top of the pile. He held the sides of the truck and pushed down hard. He went down, slowly, pushing the air out, crushing the softer parts of things, making it possible to take more on.

Next time you're doing it, he said.

When it was his turn, it was late in the day and they were full. Gene threw a final bag on top, then pointed and said *get to it*. They were stopped in the middle of a country road, at some spot in the narrows where dead trees stuck out of swamp water. Richard climbed up the gates and put himself in the middle of the load. Pushed his legs and boots into the pool of shiny green-and-black bags. It felt like it was eating him. There were a few dull pops below him, followed by a whine like something small and scared was getting suffocated. A burst of hot air rose up from below but didn't keep rising. Instead it surrounded him. Then, after a while, when he couldn't sink down further, he felt it fighting him, pushing back up, like he was the only thing keeping it in there. He imagined that if he weren't there, all of it might surge over the edges of the truck, escape into the forest and multiply.

Richard saw the worst of it late in the winter.

It happened when he wasn't sure if he could even keep doing the job. Back when he'd lost weight, and muscle too. When he'd lifted up his shirt to show his wife that the ring of fat around his middle had disappeared, and her smile only lasted as long as it took for her gaze to meet his face.

You look tired though.

I am tired, he said. Really tired.

The job was the hardest work Richard had ever done. He'd dug holes and held up sheets of drywall, demolished homes and moved them, and this was the hardest. Moving came close, but with moving there were sometimes smaller houses, or houses without much in the way of books or furniture or the things that you had to work in unison with another guy to get through a hallway and down a set of steps. And with moving, even on the hardest days, you'd have at least ten guys to blow through the work, to take the place apart and move it down the road like ants.

He and his wife had talked about whether or not it was smart to keep the job and decided that he was making more with Gene than he had at anything else he had ever done. Because she wasn't working, and there was a child on the way, even if he wanted to look for something else, it would have to wait. So there was nothing more that he or she could say, and he was careful not to complain around her.

He seemed to always have a dull headache that stayed with him so long everything seemed grey and strange, like he was in a dream. He felt empty and drained, like a shadow of himself cast upon the wall. It was in this state, early in the morning, that he tipped over a steel drum with his work gloves and saw it:

Two beach towels, decorated with the California Raisins, soaked through with blood.

They'd seen blood before. Blood was everywhere, all around them. In food and on maxi-pads; congealed in discarded bandages and wrecked clothing. Lining the brims of ballcaps and pooled in the middle of rusting duvets. But not like this, and never this much.

The towels were balled up, and after he grabbed them, something fell out into the snow and landed with a thick kind of wetness. They were at the Cliftons.

A girl's nightie, green with lace trim, dark and wet.

The blood looked fresh and red and only a bit of it gone brown, because it was partially frozen. Not even in a bag, but tossed in overtop of one, almost casually. Like it was meant to be there.

Holy shit, Richard said.

He'd grabbed it automatically, like he would have grabbed a bag, only to have it fall apart on him. And then he'd dropped it. Blood on his gloves and coveralls. A thick, congealed clot on his boot.

Oh fuck.

Throw it in, Gene said. Throw it in right now.

He had taken one look at it, accepted it for what it was, and was ready to move on. But Richard stood in the snow, still looking down at it. The purple cartoon face had gone black with blood, and the yellow saxophone was completely red. A lot of it wasn't yet unfurled. He was worried to move it, in case there was something inside, something small. He knew what it could be. His wife was five months along, and this was what they feared, what she took vitamins and drank special shakes for, was why Richard moved the cat litter outside and cleaned it himself. He was looking at what they never wanted to see. Or something even worse.

But Gene was quick to come over, grab all of it off the ground, and ball it up, another fat fleck sticking to his glove. He threw it in the back while Richard stood stone still.

Hurry the fuck up, Gene said.

They took the rest of the trash—twenty bags, far more than any one household was ever supposed to give them—with their heads down, and didn't look up at the house it had come from until they were in the truck, and moving. Both of them saw one of the curtains from the main house pull back, and drop. Gene looked away, and Richard watched. A dark shape behind a maroon blind that lingered, then moved on.

When this load was tipped, instead of watching it come out, Gene said that they had better get a move on. They pulled away from the bags they had collected and left them in an uninspected heap for the first time.

At the start of his second year with Gene, Richard's wife told him his body had changed again.

His back and shoulders had grown muscular, over-developed from throwing bags, while his biceps shrunk. All the fat was gone from his body, and his face was hollow at the cheeks and full of muscle or tendons that weren't there before. She told him—when she put his hand inside her bathrobe and onto her breast—that his hands were softer than they'd ever been.

He had worked hard to prove himself to Gene, and did it by never calling in sick, never showing up hung over, and never complaining. He worked as hard as he could through the spring thaw, when they were rained on and their feet were ice cold, and every bag was at least three times as heavy. Worked through the summer heat, when everything stunk worse than it ever had and anything left too long was busy and alive with maggots working hard to transform themselves into hard, black horseflies that bit hard enough to draw blood. By then, Richard could finally keep up with him.

Richard learned to act like Gene, to criticize the households for their shabby job of things. Used his lingo, too. Would hold up a bag full of computer parts and say, like Gene would, that these guys *were trying to pull a fast one on them* or that *they think they're sly, don't they?* They were something more than companions and less than friends, more than a boss and an employee.

By the time fall came and they were taking away leaves and pumpkin guts along with their regular loads, Richard could sense when Gene needed him. Could swoop in and give him a hand and do it wordlessly, and Gene could do the same. When a bag was stuck, in the microsecond it took to feel it sticking, one of them could grab the can and pull it free for the other in one quick motion. He had put himself inside of Gene's range of motion, too. Had built in himself a copy of Gene, a careful record of all of his movements and esti-mations, his timing and range. On the run, they were fast-moving reflections of each other that would stop, empty, throw, and leave in efficient little bursts.

Gene had remarked in small ways about Richard's development. When he achieved a long-distance throw, and the bag arced overhead with the perfect *whoosh*, Gene would give him the A-OK sign with his fingers and thumb. He would laugh with joy when Richard one-handed a heavy, bloated bag over his shoulder.

Now you're working, he'd say, and they both would smile.

But still, when they passed over the threshold to that other place, nothing had changed. Even on beautiful days, when all was quiet except for birds and trees and the sound of their small movements, something felt wrong. Richard could see it on Gene's face, an expression he knew was on his own face too: worry. It kept them quiet and, at the Clifton's, completely silent, as if a single wrong word might summon the whole clan from their nest.

When Richard finally told his wife about them, it was because of the swing set.

He had kept them from her, had kept all mention of their waste separate from their home and the people in it. Had never mentioned the blood, or the mess, or the crimes Gene had told him about. But the swings had broken this barrier for him.

It was winter, and the yard had become a maze again—even worse than before—but there was something else, too. Something at the head of all that trash, waiting for them.

When they were pulling up to it, from afar, he didn't know precisely what he was looking at, but he knew it was going to make him angry. It was a swing set, enormous with thick, metal poles—the kind you'd find at a school—maybe ten-feet tall, with cracking blue paint. Each one of its legs rested in a trash barrel, and the whole thing was leaning strangely in the snow bank, towering over them. It was so huge it couldn't fit in the truck even if it were empty and they had four guys to move it. And yet it had come here from somewhere else, had been brought here by them. How had it even made it here?

When he gazed upon it, Richard felt the same thing he'd felt before, when the roofers didn't pay him and he'd shown up on the job to collect. Not just anger, but a righteous fury that came with such a sense of certainty that he felt invulnerable. If the men on the roof, all of them holding hammers, had come after him, he imagined their blows would have bounced right off him. He felt the same now, like if the Cliftons came out all at once he could pull them apart with his bare hands.

When they got out, both men stood and looked at it for a while. It had no seats, just hanging chains, clinking like wind chimes.

After Richard jerked at the legs and found that he couldn't even budge them in the cans, he laughed:

Are you fucking serious?

Gene pinched between his eyebrows. He spoke quietly, with his eyes closed:

We have to find a way to take this.

Why not just go talk to them? Richard asked, knowing the answer, feeling something sour blooming inside of himself.

No, Gene said with some effort. Just leave it be.

They had gone through this in the fall, when the Cliftons put out an entire shower stall with a toilet inside of it. It was smashed and sliding around in four big pieces, and Gene accepted this without question, took on the extra load as if any other course of action were impossible. Richard protested for the first time by asking if they *really* had to take it, but did it while helping to heave it up and over the second closed gate.

Don't you get sick of this shit? Richard asked him.

Gene swallowed instead of answering, then wiped his forehead.

Ten minutes later the stall came off the back and tumbled onto the road. They stopped, not to heave it back onto the pile, but to shove it down into a ditch. It landed in thick mud and reeds, on its side. Gene felt satisfied leaving it like that.

We can just say we didn't notice it go, he told Richard. If anybody asks.

And Richard watched as it collected brown water from the little brook flowing through the ditch before he moved on.

With the swing set, Richard decided that if it were still there when they came back the next week, he would go and talk to them, with or without Gene. When the truck shuddered around the corner, and they saw it for the second time, it had taken on new shape. With the snow bank at its side, all the new bags of waste had collected against the swing set and on top of it, giving it new mass. Richard thought it looked like a temple in the making, somewhere you'd sacrifice virgins to the spirits circling overhead. With the Cliftons' garbage cans out of commission, more bags than usual had been left out and torn open. Crows were eating what was left.

Richard felt something familiar.

It pulled him out of the truck, past all the fleeing birds, and onto the property itself. It moved him through the rotting fence and past two speakers, stripped of their foam, sitting next to a gutted dryer, the little pieces of litter probably thrown directly from the house. Then he was up and onto the porch, a mess of trash and snow and ice and junk either too difficult to get out onto the yard or into the house. Two frozen couches, a china cabinet without doors. A set of aluminum blinds twisted and wrapped around a red snow-blower blade. There was warm air blowing out from inside the house. Richard realized he was knocking on the door.

A dog barked.

He waited.

When it opened, the old man was there, smoking a cigarette, looking sickly thin, like a mummy in long johns. He didn't say hello or ask any questions. He crumpled the checkerboard of lines on his forehead and made his eyes disappear in a squint.

Listen, Richard heard himself say. You gotta get this thing outta here.

He looked past Richard, and searched in the distance. A smile opened his face back up and he laughed when he saw the mound.

The boys put that out. He shook his head. I told them you fellas wouldn't take it but they didn't listen.

We can take five bags from most households. For you guys, we do more. But we can't take your swing set.

Well, he said, his smile leaving him. You gotta take it.

We can't take it.

Whatever we give you, you take it. You put it in that little truck and you go. It's your job to take it.

Actually it isn't, Richard said. It *is* a little truck, though, you're right. And we can only take so much. And this is too much.

Who says it's too much? He looked at him. You? There are fourteen of us.

He peered with one burning eye at the road, at Gene, looking small in the driver's seat. He pointed with a knobby finger.

Does he decide?

Then there was silence except for the wind sucking the smell out from the house. Richard clenched his jaw and swallowed before speaking.

We can't even move the thing.

You take what we give you, he said.

You get that out of there or else we can't take any of your trash. Period.

The two stood for a moment, looking into each other's eyes.

Then, Richard tried again:

We can go to the county, he said. Go and get a fine for all this.

Is that the truth? Can you?

We can, Richard said.

Well, the old man said, we'll see.

He shut the door.

When he crunched back to Gene through the snow and saw him trying to pull a garbage bag off the top of the mound, Richard told him to stop, and Gene did. He brought his arms down to his sides, slowly, then looked to Richard, who told him to get back in the truck. Gene obeyed, because things were different now.

It all changed when Richard surpassed Gene.

When he was faster and used to the system and terrain and could act before a need even arose. It was when Gene had him back to the garage and sat him next to the little wood stove again after they were back from the run. The truck parked next to them, grey and dented and covered in a film of grease that was cleaned off only once a year.

I could write my name in that, Richard thought.

Gene spoke at length about what good a job Richard had been doing, and offered him a raise. He had brought him there expressly for this purpose, and was frank about it:

I've given two guys a raise, and it was only ever after a good five years or so, he said. But I'm older now and you help me a hell of a lot. So I thought I'd let you know I want to pay you more, if the idea is that you want to keep doing this.

I do, Richard said. I want to keep doing this, Gene.

Well then, that sounds good to me.

They shook hands then, and sat inside of what seemed like happiness.

The change came later, in Richard's mind. When it occurred to him for the first time that all of this was malleable. That they could get people to follow the rules if they really wanted to, if they weren't afraid. That Gene could spend a quarter of the money he spent on his raise and get a new truck. Or a second one. That they could split the work between them and be finished faster, spread it out over one extra day and not have to work so hard. That this whole operation hinged on the fact that Gene wanted four days straight to do whatever the fuck he needed all those hours for.

The next time he saw Gene, it had become something he could feel. A difference in balance, in the space between them. He didn't have a word for what was gone. When he and Gene emptied cans in unison, put them down, and went their separate ways to the driver's and passenger's side, it was something missing in their movements. A tug.

He came up with the word looking into his son's mouth, wet with orange mush, at his lips and the ridge of pink where his teeth were beginning to sprout. He thought of the name of what had been between them that was now gone, or else something that was imaginary and never there to begin with.

Tether, he said.

When Richard walks towards the Clifton house for the last time, Gene stays in the truck and waits. The pyramid is nearly a complete, missing only a few blocks near its middle. A mound of garbage nearly big enough to necessitate its own run to the sorting centre. Its chains no longer clinking, but resting on a heap of taut, black bags.

This time, Richard knocks on the door with enough force that he feels it give a little.

This time, he receives no answer.

He waits, and knocks again. Looks to his left. Just past the porch, a picnic table beside a mound of dirt. A hole nearby with half a motorcycle in it.

As he waits, he starts to deflate. He feels Gene's gaze burning into the back of his head, a hot tickle.

Finally he turns around, and leaves. Goes down the steps and begins to walk back. He sees that Gene's face is turned in his direction, but it's looking past him, at the house. Richard turns just in time to see the door shutting, and something shoot out. At first he doesn't know what he's looking at because it's bright, and all he can hear is the wind.

It's black and low to the ground, coming at him like a tiny storm cloud.

He realizes it's a dog when it's close enough to open its mouth, and by then it is too late to run, or really do anything. All he can do is offer up his hand in place of his neck or face or crotch, and the mouth accepts, taking it on with ease. Then it has him, and they are one, a man with a black dog on the end of his arm. Richard holds his own wrist, trying to pry himself free, and trying to kick the dog, too.

From the truck, it looks like they're dancing. It sounds like Richard's singing, crying out in whoops and hollers, even though he isn't. It takes a long time before Gene is able to move, to unclick his seatbelt, and open the door, heave his weight from the seat and rush forward. For a while he watches them through his own clouded breath on the window before he opens the door.

After Gene finally gets to him, a heavy flat-head shovel clenched between his gloved fingers, it still takes twenty more minutes.

Gene swings, sometimes hitting the dog, sometimes hitting the ground. When he does connect and the metal ricochets off the dog's skull, pain shoots through Richard's whole body and he cries out. Eventually Gene gives up with the shovel, grabs the dog by the hind legs and pulls back with all his strength, kicks at its underside, but it won't let go. Richard grabs at whatever he can find littered on the ground. Snow and clumps of dead grass. An empty cloth pencil case. An old bleach container, stomped flat. A paint can lid. The chewed-up remote control from a toy car. A six-inch length of garden hose. At one point he tries to grab something round and red and comes away with nothing, realizing it's his own blood. His scavenger hunt ends when his hand falls on the curved end of a broken cinderblock with real weight to it, fifteen feet from where this started.

The dog releases him after five blows to its snout and head, but Richard doesn't allow it to retreat. Instead, he is up and the shovel is in his hands—in both the good hand and the ruined one—and he's swinging it harder than Gene ever could. Chasing after it. The dog takes more blows to the skull as it tries to run away, yelping and staggering with each one. It's knocked over and silenced completely when the shovel is swung sideways into the bone of its neck with a hard snap. After it's down, after it has stopped opening and closing its jaws, and even after its black lips have drawn back down over its teeth, Richard doesn't stop. He's working harder than he's ever worked, bringing the shovel up and down, up and down onto the dark body lying in the yard with all the other things.

Later, when Richard bursts through the Cliftons' door with his hand dangling at his side and Gene following him, he hasn't slowed any. He charges through the cold room and into a hallway with fake wood panelling, blue shag carpet. Stacks of dead TVs and radios and record players, all pushed up against a wall. Crosses into what looks like a living room.

There, five children sit on a rug before a television, five bowls of cereal before them, their faces lit by a dull warbling. One boy, maybe the oldest, maybe nine years old, upright and leaning against the couch, looking out of place and awkward as he searches their faces.

Richard goes to move, to search the kitchen and back and upstairs, but the entire motion is short circuited into a sort of twitch.

He stops. Gene is saying his name.

That's when he realizes it, and feels it. A big feeling, so big it's like he's standing on it. He remembers outside, the van—the one he'd seen the children and the women piling into—up on blocks and under a tarp. And there were none of the usual trucks or rusting cars parked haphazardly across the lot. He looks at a child's pale face, flickering blue from the light of the television, the only light in the house. They're alone. The only adults are he and Gene, together in the dark. No one's in charge. Not on this floor, or in this house, or on this parcel of land. Not anywhere along this road, not even where it ends and branches out in every direction, like lightning.

GIRL ON FIRE ESCAPE

I MET HER at a party for cam girls and cam boys. People who jerk themselves off in front of webcams for other people to watch. So that they can jerk themselves off too. If they have a credit card.

At least that's what I thought it was. I had seen cam-girls before on pop-up ads, the kind you click away from because they cost money or give you viruses or keep you from getting to the *real* porn, and all I had ever seen in those windows were grainy, pixellated hands fiddling with grainy, pixellated crotches. At the party they explained that it was mostly a performance directed by the audience—a bunch of people (men) demanding this and that in a chat window—and anything could happen. Show your ass, show your tits, put oil on them. Use the blue dildo. No, the other blue dildo, with the real-looking head and balls. Now the big red butt plug shaped like an atomic bomb. The combinations were endless.

Marc, who cleans high-rise windows with me, was dating a girl who did cams for a living. Her name was Leslie and even though I met her only once, she had made it her job to find me a girlfriend. It was the first thing she said to me. Her, in a sweatsuit and without makeup, me in my soap-stained company uniform, sitting across from each other while Marc rooted around for rolling papers. She asked:

Do you have anybody yet?

As if being alone isn't even a choice to be made, a default setting I was waiting to move past. But I said what she wanted to hear, which was *no not yet*, so she was able to get started right there on the couch, counting off the girls on her clicking corn-chip-sized fingernails. Marc said it was her way of making a little family out of us, to try and get some double dates and game nights going. She was new to the city like I was, Marc explained, and she got lonely. I said it sounded to me like she had lots of friends. Or fans, anyway. He didn't like that.

I almost didn't go to the party. I had to clean a building in the morning and had decided I wouldn't attend since I was in the dish pit at the restaurant that night too. Washing and bussing glasses and mugs and dishes— hundreds and hundreds of them until my hands were red and raw and ready to flake apart like puff pastry— and also drinking.

Finding and consuming abandoned drinks wasn't exactly allowed, but no one ever stopped us from doing it. The servers, who were repulsed by what we did— who could afford to buy their own drinks and disguise them as coffee in travel mugs—weren't able to tattle because they were just as guilty. Untouched, or hardly touched, was my only rule—a rule that kept me relatively sober—but that night six businessmen walked out with a fresh round of Guinness on the table, and I was able to get there in time, get them back to the dish pit, and line them up side by side, right at eye level, on the shelf of cleaning supplies before anyone stopped me. By the time I ruined the perfect white head and sucked in the warm, black body of the last one, the choice had been made for me.

Leslie's name got me in the door, but no one was happy about it, because I was in my whites, unshaven and unshowered and smelling like six perfect pints. The woman who let me in was wearing a sparkling silver dress and long white gloves like Miss America. The others were in cocktail dresses and gowns, two were in latex or rubber dresses, purple-black like a balloon. There were maybe fourteen people there, standing around this open-concept loft, drinking in their uncomfortable thick-as-phonebook shoes, watching a porno movie projected on the wall. I had to duck to the bathroom to make myself presentable, to use their handsoap on my armpits and strip down to my t-shirt, wet my hair and try to make myself even the tiniest bit like them.

It was a launch party for a website, something Leslie and Marc had failed to mention. There were little cards everywhere that said SensualCams VIP Pass that sort of came apart like a scratch ticket. A balloon girl asked me:

Are you excited to go live?

And I said *yes I am*.

Marc and Leslie had also failed to show up, though I might've seen them on the overhead. I definitely saw Leslie—naked and rocking back and forth on someone's face—in what I realized was a repeating loop of performances that made up an ad. In it, her eyes were painted in thick, black strokes like a Pharaoh's, and she had heavy, pyramid-shaped earrings hanging from her lobes that swung in time with her tits. I might've seen Marc's hairy belly and chin, but not his dick, which was lost between his big, fast-pumping hand and dangling scrotum. It looked, not like he was masturbating, but like he was jangling a bunch of coins in a sack. Like he was judging by weight how many quarters he'd have for laundry day.

I knew I was supposed to be turned on, and had been turned on the entire time I was in the steam of the dish pit, when everything was soft and uncertain in my mind. But when I was there, I didn't feel much of anything. I stuck with the girl in the silver dress because she had been nice enough to let me in and did her best to make me feel welcome despite it being clear I didn't belong. And even though I knew we were in her studio, and that she fucked herself just a few feet away—on the little foam couch with a white sheet pinned to the wall, by the flood lamp on a tripod—it didn't change anything. Even the row of dildos along the windowsill weren't tantalizing. They were just sort of there, just like the shampoos and body washes and hair products that were in her bathroom.

I decided that, on my own, everything had been uncertain, but here, nothing was. I spent the first while trying to match up the performer and the performer's code name on the overhead with the people in the room, which was the closest I could get to any sort of mystery. Searching among the stockings and cleavage for Sephora and Valkyrie, Speedy Rider and ~Double D Goddess~. Eventually I remembered why I was here and asked our host (JungleJenny) if she knew which one was Veronica.

Our boss didn't show up, so people left, she said. She might've been here. But I wouldn't know her real name anyway.

I removed myself from the main room when I realized I was standing alone, feeling both out of place and not there at all. Like the way you are in a dream, a pair of eyes, just watching. That's when I went from being Moody Guy Nobody Knows to the Guy On Fire Escape.

And that's where she was, drinking from a wine bottle.

She wore one of those glittery wigs—colour and texture obviously fake—but cut so it fit her. It was blue with silver bits, tight on her head. She was pale, and the wig brought out the veins from under her skin.

Instead of saying hello she said this was her spot, and I told her I didn't know anyone was out here.

I am someone and I am here, she said.

I was going to leave when she started looking me over, which let me do the same to her. She was beautiful, but everyone here was too, so it almost meant nothing. She had tattoos, which also should have meant nothing, but hers were different. After a second I saw that it was actually only one, not several; something isolated to the centre of her chest, spreading up from between her breasts to her collarbones, stopping just before her throat. Big and complicated and colourful with birds and hearts and an all-seeing eye. It looked ancient and powerful, full of detailed line-work like something from a tarot card.

She asked if I was one of them, and motioned inside.

Do I look like one of them? I asked.

No, but you could be. You could be anyone. Are you a cook?

I lied and said yes. I asked if she worked for the website and she pointed at the humping flesh on the wall.

I squinted to see a pair of wide hips pumping up and down on some guy with an electric-orange tan and tube socks. There was a huge, white scar up the centre of her. A Caesarean.

That's you? I asked.

She drank instead of answering.

I squinted again and when I looked back at her, she was still drinking from her bottle, staring down into the brick neighbourhood.

I asked if she was Veronica. She laughed and said she was more of a Betty than a Veronica. She kept drinking.

I asked her if it was okay if I smoked.

No, she said. It's not okay.

I pointed at her bottle and told her that wasn't any better for her.

What? She smiled, and tilted the bottle towards me. Grape Juice?

Something about the way she answered bothered me and I felt myself starting to leave. But then her hand was on my arm. She said she was going anyway. Stepped back into the apartment, but poked her head back outside, and I felt all that frustration leave me when her eyes locked with mine.

I'm Gretchen, she said.

I didn't know if that was her real name or her code name so I told her mine was Ace, and she shook my moistureless hand, her eyes still locked on me. I asked if I could call her.

I can't give you my number, she said. I don't have one.

Do you have Facebook?

No I don't have Facebook.

Oh.

After a moment, she raised her eyebrows, her wig raising with them.

Do you know what a dead drop is? She asked.

No.

It's a kind of mailbox we both check. I don't have a phone but I use a dead drop. Do you want to know where it is?

I felt stupid again, like I was being fucked with, but her face lit up when she saw I was thinking it over. Finally I said yeah, I want to know, and she explained hers was in an alley behind a place called Foolhardy's on Queen Street. In a wall overtop the dumpster. She explained that there was a mural of a bunch of dragons, and the dead drop was in a hole in the centre of the yellow dragon's eye.

You can roll up a piece of paper and put it in there, she said. Can you remember all that?

I said I could, which was all she needed to hear in order to leave.

I was out there for a long time before I remembered I was there to smoke. When I finished my cigarette, I picked up her bottle of wine. There was no label to speak of. I took a swig.

It was sweet and mild and made my heart race.

Grape juice.

I took a VIP PASS on the way out.

When I got up the next day I was still thinking about her. I went to the website before I got dressed, holding the erection I'd woken up with, trying to save it for her. Tore open the ticket and put in the code. I kept clicking from window to window looking for something of her in those tiny thumbnails. Blue hair. Her tattoo. A face that made me feel something thicken in my chest.

Finally I found that vertical scar and a chest scribbled in ink and I clicked on it. She was doing a backwards cowgirl, two strong male hands on her hips. But when she brought her open mouth and big eyes up to the webcam, I could plainly see it wasn't Gretchen. She seemed too happy. Or maybe too nice. I kept flicking back and forth through the different cams, looking for her. A lot of the girls were just sitting, clothed, waiting for someone to come into the room, brushing their hair, fixing their cleavage. I found Leslie in a pair of argyle socks and nothing else. She was sitting in her living room, in the same chair I had sat in, with her bare legs up against her chest, her arms around her knees, a piece of toast hanging from her hand. She was looking at something off camera and rubbing her nose every so often. Smoke was coming up from an ashtray somewhere beside her.

In the dish pit, I gave the card to Diego, who became deadly serious about the whole matter. He touched the little cartoon woman on the card with all four fingers like she was a saint. This is nice website, man.

I told him I knew someone who worked for them. He nodded seriously, steam rising all around us.

This looks like a very fucking hot site, bro. How much?

It's yours, I said.

I will use this, he grinned. I will get some use out of this gift, bro, let me tell you.

I always knew what Diego was thinking or feeling because he never let anything stay inside himself. Everything just poured out of him. It didn't matter if it was stupid or crude or embarrassing, because no one, not the servers or the managers or even the cooks listened to him. He could let loose everything inside of himself and fill up the entire basement with the sound of his thoughts and no one could hear it except me.

This time was all about how he'd have to figure out some way to watch the shows alone. His wife was pregnant with his third child and wasn't fucking him, something he'd mentioned every shift for a month now. This time, he left out the part about her placenta being on a dangerous angle, something that might put the baby at risk if they fucked. This fact had fallen out of him one time, when he came to work sad and somber, and was never repeated again. Instead, he'd settled into a routine of complaining about her that he didn't seem to be able to control, that sprayed out of him like it was on a timer.

He held two steel-wool scouring pads to his crotch, cupping them like they were heavy. My balls are like this, man.

I told him mine were too, and he punched me, asked what her name was.

All I could do was shrug because I wasn't even sure.

Of course, there was no dead drop. There was no bar called Foolhardy's either. The dumpster and the dragon mural and the other stuff were all there, but I only found it by trudging through a mile of alleyways stinking with trash. The wall and the yellow dragon's eye were smooth with plaster. I was balanced on top of two trashcans feeling around for it when I realized it. Then a window opened two floors up across from me and I fell down.

It was her.

She was leaning out the window in a blue t-shirt, her hair—her real hair—looking sort of dull and cropped close, like she'd recently shaved it.

Ace, she said.

I picked myself up and said Gretchen.

She said that wasn't her name. Now her name was Katja.

She asked why I came and I asked her what *she* thought I was there for.

You're here to try and fuck me, she guessed. Or make me your girlfriend. Make me do something you saw me do on the internet.

You weren't on that website, I shouted up to her.

I'm in the fine print on the legal page.

Then she thought about it, and decided to laugh at me: You actually joined?

I felt another wave of embarrassment and it must've shown. She laughed even harder.

I thought (but didn't say) that I wasn't going to stand there and take this. But I did. Waited through a minute of laughter.

You want to go on a date, huh? She said in a mocking tone. You wanna fall in love?

Yeah, I said, I do.

Fine, she said. Let's fall in love.

We went to a nearby place called Frankie's that she said she went to every day.

I started to order breakfast but she told me to stop, waved away the server, who called her Tonya, not Gretchen.

She explained that this wasn't the date. The date hadn't started yet. Then she pointed at some candy machine next to a jukebox. Told me to listen up.

There were over five hundred Vendco vending machines on the west side of the city alone, in malls and bus stations, stadiums and restaurants, bars, grocery stores, ranging in size from those little gumball dispensers to towering snack machines. She pointed to an extra-long cargo van parked out front that we were going to fill. Then she showed me a bunch of keys, one for every machine's padlock, labelled with dirty bits of tape and yellow paper and on a big silver ring. Unlock them, take the machines away, tell whoever asked that we're repairing them, easy-peasy. We would only take them from big, busy areas, never small businesses where they might know the owners. Katja wanted fifteen gumball-style machines, two drink machines, and one snack machine.

I asked why but she said there was no why. I had more questions but I could see there was no point in asking.

You don't want to? She asked. You're okay with the cams, but not this?

So you are a cam girl?

I'm mostly just the accountant now, she said, then motioned around her. And this.

And what's this?

A person who takes things, stupid.

Once we got in the truck she wanted to know if I had a record. I said I didn't, but I'm not sure if that's what she wanted to hear.

She said I needed a name because she wasn't calling me Ace all night.

I put on a real hard scowl and said my name was Tony, but she just laughed and pinched my cheek.

Aww. Tony's from the wrong side of the tracks? Had a hard life, has he?

He has. He actually really has.

Ooo, she raised her eyebrows. Dangerous.

I went to light a cigarette and she told me Tony doesn't smoke.

I told her he does, and she took my cigarette and lighter and said he doesn't. Especially not in Katja's van.

The Vendco job went off without a hitch. No one asked what we were doing, the little machines were easy to carry, and the big ones weren't hard to manage once you got them on the dolly. Katja was as tall as me, which I hadn't realized until now. Just as strong, maybe stronger. Smarter. When we walked side by side, we didn't feel like a couple. It was more like we were partners. A few times I tried to reach over and touch her arm, but she was all business. I was told to focus.

It started out as an exciting thing to do, and the both of us were full of energy. It was like all the feelings I had expected to feel at the party were there with me. I vibrated in my seat, and everything she said was funny and sharp and witty and I was on fire. But little by little, as we completed more of the work, it just sort of became another job. I started to remember that I knew nothing about her, that she knew nothing about me, and that my being with her was probably a bad idea.

When we were done she parked in the alley and made me wait at the entrance to keep a look out while she went around to the back. I heard her screwing around with the machines, clinking and clanking for almost a half hour. When she finally closed the door, she came over to me with heavy plastic grocery bags. Three triple-bagged sacs filled with quarters and two filled with jellybeans, roasted peanuts, chocolate-covered raisins, and little plastic blisters with prizes inside. She made me take them, hold them steady in front of myself. When we kissed, she put both hands on the bags like they were part of me.

I wanted to smoke afterwards, sweaty and exhausted on her mattress, the taste of her still in my mouth. She didn't tell me not to, but she asked if I would wait. She even said please. When I said I would, she thanked me. She got up to make us tea, pushing aside a hanging sheet to head into her kitchenette. It was a bachelor's apartment, but she'd strung up shower curtains and swatches of fabric to divide everything up.

She did have a scar on her stomach, but it was going in the wrong direction. I kept looking at it, touching it. That, and her tattoo. It was huge, and even more complex than I thought. Now that it was uncovered I could see that the flowers and flames and birds were all coming from a huge, flaming bird, spitting fire upwards to the eye. There was a banner with something in Latin. I asked her what it meant and she said *memento mori*, which answered nothing.

She gave me tea and asked me on another date. Frankie's Pub again, by the insane asylum.

I asked if that's where she came from but she didn't laugh.

That's not funny, she answered.

Happiness left me. I didn't like the way she could move back and forth between the things she'd made up and the things she actually felt, or the way she could wield either of them against me. When I'd asked what she needed the machines for, she said they were for her father, for Father's Day. All of my excitement was gone too, and underneath it, I had anger for her.

I asked her why she was like this.

She shook her head solemnly and put my hands on her breasts. She declared that she lost both of them to cancer but had survived and now every day was a gift.

I tried to sidestep her nonsense by looking into her eyes, sternly, and telling her my name was Chris. That I was twenty-two years old and from Charlottetown. That I came here after dropping out of college because I was all fucked up.

She saw that I was giving her something of myself and softened a little. Clarified that she didn't actually lose her tits. But she did come back from the dead.

Then I asked it as quietly as I could. Maybe so she couldn't hear what was in my voice.

What's your real name?

Gretchen, she said.

Really?

She shrugged, and that's what did it. That was all I could take. I left.

She said she loved me as I got dressed, but in a nonchalant kind of way, her legs crossed, still holding a saucer and a teacup over her naked body. Said it like it was something she said all the time. From the window she called down.

I love you Tony. I love you Chris.

The Sobey's bags were so full I could hardly lift them, and I lost a lot of quarters and candy going up the street. I realized on the bus that I'd forgotten my workbag, my wallet and uniform, but I wasn't going back to get them.

Diego and I ate big handfuls from the bags between sips of a Corona we'd split. He drank leftovers like I did, and ate them too, but only if they came from women. He was telling me about how his wife found the VIP PASS in his pants and tore it up in front of him. He wanted to know if I could get him another. I was in the middle of telling him I couldn't get him another one when our little Iranian boss came downstairs. Told us to get back to work. Clapping his hands violently to signal that it had to be *now*, and clapping so hard that any excuses I tried to get out were squashed between his palms.

I grabbed my bin and ran up the stairs, keeping time with him. As I opened the door to the restaurant, he grabbed my arm and explained that someone was there to see me, but I couldn't meet them until I cleared all the dishes and was on my break, fifteen minutes away.

Do you understand? He asked, still holding my arm like you'd hold a toddler's.

She sat at a table near the front, a kerchief around her head and big sunglasses like a movie star on the lam, white fur coat and those one-size-fit-all cotton gloves, bare legs shining under the dim lights. She looked fake and weird, but fit in perfectly with the place's Tex-Mex decor. Her back was against the painted wall, the one with a cactus and a sunset and a sombreroed man on a donkey.

I motioned for her to go around into the alley behind the restaurant, gathered as many dishes as I could in one go, went downstairs, and out the emergency exit. Diego asked what I was doing but I ignored him.

All I could smell were the dumpsters and her perfume. When she said hello, she called me by my real name. I told her I still didn't know what to call her. She put her hand on my cheek, but those gloves and those sunglasses made it so I couldn't feel or see anything of her. I told her to take that shit off, so she removed her big fur coat and tossed it on the ground, dramatically. Then she came over and pressed her body to me and kissed my neck even though my arms were at my sides and not around her. Kissed me even though I smelled like sweat and brown water and had spinach-artichoke dip speckled across me.

I like you, she said.

I looked down and away from her but she took my face, started petting it.

I just need a yes or no.

Yes or no to what?

She told me she was getting out of the city, and she wanted me to come with her.

She lifted her glasses to say it, so I could see she was serious. But then she took out a gun from her waistband and held it up, her eyes darting around. I could see it was plastic, could see the orange tip on the end.

Shit's about to go down, she said. Her kerchief fluttered.

Will you stop? I asked.

I'm not joking you know.

There's something wrong with you, I said.

She pointed the gun at the dish-pit window. Leaves blew by.

And what about that? She asked. Nothing's wrong with that?

I couldn't see him, but I knew Diego was inside, looking up at our feet. At her legs, unable to pull his gaze away. Imagining his face between her thighs, or maybe those legs wrapped around him. Maybe still working, maybe not, waiting for the day to be over but unable to leave.

She didn't say anything else. Just showed me her hands, palms up, her fingers still wrapped around the gun, her gloves against the plastic. I went back inside, and she went back down the alley against the wind.

Maybe two days later I saw Leslie.

Marc and I were cleaning a food court's skylight, a job that kept us focused enough that we didn't talk much. It was a big honeycomb that collected bird shit and fat, juicy spiders that we had to kill and scrape off before we could even start squeegeeing. Before we started, I said to Marc:

Did nobody think of how hard this would be to clean?

And he said *Nope* in a way that made me sound naïve for even thinking it.

Leslie appeared behind the glass breezeway where the access door was. She looked halfway between what I'd seen on the wall at the party, and how she looked when I first met her, wearing sweatpants and sneakers, a wide-open windbreaker, and what looked like a piece of lingerie for a top. Her face was streaked in lines of makeup sludge and my first thought was that someone had died.

Jesus fucking Christ, said Marc.

He threw his rag down and went towards her, but lost any menace along the way. We knew the glass wasn't loadbearing so he had to crab walk along the steel frame in order to get to her, which could only ever look silly.

How did she find us? I called to him.

But then he was up and inside the breezeway and with her.

I kept working, but glanced up at them every now and then. There was a space and distance between the two of them, and I could see that they just weren't on the same level anymore. She hugged herself, and he motioned a lot, pointed and waved his hands. Even without the reactions of the people going by, it was clear they were fighting. It occurred to me that Marc looked exhausted—had looked exhausted all day—like this had been going on for some time.

When it was finally over, and he crawled back over to his spot, his face was red, the bags under his eyes swollen like he'd aged and turned into the person he'd be ten years from now. Still cleaning windows but with all joy and vitality wrung out of him. Leslie sat on the breezeway floor like she'd collapsed that way, stayed there for another half hour. I made a point not to look her way, because seeing her made me feel sad and guilty and sort of scooped-out on the inside. I was also careful not to press Marc, but on the elevator, when we were leaving the job three hours later, he was compelled to tell me.

Sensualcams.com lost a lot of money and had to let go of every cam girl except the top twenty. Marc said Leslie was in the top thirty-five (which sounded to me like she was #35 on the nose) and had just missed the cut-off. Someone who handled the credit cards and Paypal accounts had taken and sold all that information, emptied the funds for advertising, PR, and found some way to drink the entirety of the company's savings and their by-the-minute earnings on top of that.

She doesn't know what she's going to do, Marc said, because she quit her real job to do this and they probably won't take her back.

He added:

I didn't want her doing this shit anyway.

I asked—carefully—about the person who did it to them. Do they know who it is, and did they get caught?

Marc said that the person was a girl named Gretchen. We were down in the street by then, making our way home.

If anyone sees her again, he said, she's a dead person.

The next day I almost left Frankie's five times waiting for her. My hands were shaking, and my teeth chattered. A homeless man in a coonskin cap kept whispering swears in my ear and asking me if I was a Freemason. We sat together and I bought us each a four-dollar breakfast with handfuls of quarters.

When she showed up I almost didn't recognize her. She was wearing jeans and sneakers, but they were frayed and stained. She wore an old poker visor, lime green, and those same huge sunglasses. She looked like a street person.

I told Davey Crockett to give me a minute and he shook my hand, arranging our thumbs in what he explained was the grip of an entered apprentice.

She took off her sunglasses and sat down.

I didn't think. I'd promised myself I wouldn't think. I'd only speak. I can't even remember what I said. I think I was trying to argue with her, or trying to make her feel bad. Trying to make her give me something of her, like I had done with myself. I wanted her to beg me to come with her, to give me her offer, but she didn't. She sat, and listened, and waited.

Then, when I was done, she extended her arms, extended them to the people working and the people drinking and said this is it. Do it or don't.

I think if I hadn't gone after her that day, I would've gotten up the next morning and masturbated. Tried to think of anyone but her. Then I would've had a big coffee from Second Cup and climbed a ten-storey building with Will or Desmond or maybe the new guy. I would've hung over the edge on a little seat, in my harness, water and soap dripping from my squeegee down to the streets below, and I would've watched for a big green hat or a blue wig or a woman emanating an aura of power like a phoenix. I would think about her lying down, bare-chested, and having that needle score her body. Think about the way her blood must've collected around the needle before getting wiped away. Think about what she must have thought or felt when she first took off her bandages and stood before the mirror and saw herself.

I'd do this involuntarily, and when I realized it, I would try to stop. Try to move my thoughts to where I need them. Stay focused on the windows and the soap in the bucket. The perfect "S" motion to clean the whole thing in one go.

IS ALIVE AND CAN MOVE

I'D MADE IT through a real rough patch, and so I had to do everything I could to try and get something going that would keep me together. My brother wouldn't let me stay with him but he did put up the money so I could get an apartment. Said he'd help me more if I started going to meetings, but I said I didn't need that shit. Said all I needed was a job, and believed it, too. Eventually I'm hired to do cleanup at one wing of a building at the far end of the university campus. Mostly dorm rooms, but there was a cafeteria and a kitchen, a daycare, and two floors of offices for the teachers. I had to clean from midnight until it was done, which was usually five in the morning. For the first time in years, I really tried to stay on top of it and do a good job because I really had nothing else.

I held on, even though for the first week I had to smoke every five minutes, take a dump every two, and was sweating so much I looked like I'd been out in the rain. But the cleaning boss, Charles, seemed to understand. He had one of those big, bloated noses and you could see he'd been through some rough patches himself. You can never know how bad someone else has had it, but even the worst drinkers didn't have it as bad as me. I was a special case—even the doctor said so—but it was still nice to know he had an idea or two about it.

One time, he even asked how I was handling it, like he knew what it was all about, and I'd said *good*, because it was mostly true. The job gave me a place to be at the exact time most everyone would be going downtown to drive drinks into them. And it was a job that, for the most part, was quiet and didn't involve other people. Sometimes I'd see a college kid or two, shuffling around in their pajamas, but that was it. And the only other people I'd see were the professors, a couple of young ones who would even talk to me sometimes. They seemed to always be working late, smoking pipes and cigars and laughing a lot. I never really let myself get in too close, because I felt how bad they wanted me to, which could only be dangerous. I had felt something like it before, in the past, when someone was stuck themselves and wanted to draw me in for no reason except not to be alone in their situation or habit. With them, I'd allow myself a quick hello but keep moving because it was the only way I knew not to get snared.

It was impossible to start the shift at the dormitory end, because any day of the week the kids would be going right until three or four in the morning, and if you cleaned it too early, you'd have to pick up trash, mop up drinks or even puke, broken glass, shredded papers, then come back and do it all over again. Instead you'd start with the offices, go down each floor, sweep, mop, and buff. Change garbages. Vacuum the mats near the doors. Clean walls once a week. Wipe down doorknobs and railings and light switches with disinfectant. Do the toilets and sinks and stock everything up, too.

Charles said I had it right. That it was best never to even see the kids, to never even lay eyes on them. A guy who had my job from before, a few years ago, he got fired for fucking one of the girls.

"Whether or not he even did," Charles said, "And I fucking tell you he *did not* so keep that in mind, too, young fella."

One night I did end up seeing a girl, at maybe quarter to four, hanging over the stairwell, watching me polish the floor. Her tits were dangling down at me in her silvery shirt and I had to do everything not to take a second look at her. Problem was it was summer, it was hot, and we were both stripped down to almost nothing. I had on shorts and a muscle shirt, and she had on that party top, which barely covered her. Even with the noise from the polisher and all the space between us, I swear I could almost *feel* her body against mine. Smell her. It had been so long since I'd been with a woman, I almost dropped that big hand-operated thing down the stairs a dozen times.

The first thing she'd said was *you're hot* and then *you're younger than the other guy,* and *I like your tattoos.* Then she moved onto *hey* and *what's your name,* which she shouted a half-dozen times. Shouted them right down on top of me so they bounced off every surface, jumped over the buffer and into my ears.

And to be honest, I was scared, scared all around. For my job and my life and to even be seen with her. But I was most scared of what she might think if I actually went for it, if she got a good look at my face and my eyes and smelled the stink coming out of my pores. So I put my head down and pushed hard on the handles, as hard as I could, got out of there with the job half done, my shorts soaked with sweat and my chest filled up with panic.

So I kept away from there until the very end of the night for both those reasons, and because the only way for things to get back to normal was for me not to lay eyes on any bottles, not to even smell the stuff or look at it. I knew I couldn't even look at someone when they were screwed up and having a time. Doctor told me I had to do whatever I had to do in order to make it work, and the old guys who'd been able to quit altogether said shit like *it never gets easier*, and I had to believe it because what else could I believe? Even all the pamphlets said the same thing, and I'd imagined that the meetings would too.

Being alone might not have been the solution I needed, though for the first part, it was. When my system was changing, trying to turn itself—like the doctor said—from a machine that ran on grain alcohol into one that ran on food and water, I needed to be alone. When I would have sudden bursts of energy and the air smelled fresh, when all I wanted to do was tell the world how beautiful it was, when I was so emotional the taste of Mike and Ikes nearly moved me to tears, I knew it was good no one was around. Same as when I'd have a real downward dip and I would be so angry at absolutely nothing—angry at dirt and streaks and myself and the walls—those were times it was good to be alone. Then when I'd have a blackout and I'd come out of it, scared and confused, and I would have a moment where I wasn't sure if it was a new day or one that happened a long time ago. Those were times I was glad to be alone.

And then other times it would've helped to have someone there. Part of drinking so much that your brain is permanently fucked means that you have trouble staying focused on tasks, or else you can get distracted from the ones you need to be doing by ones that don't matter. For a while I got to counting all the bricks at eye level and got to thinking that if the number of bricks came out odd, it was an omen that things were going downhill again. I'd feel grim and grey and once even thought about opening one of those big, green windows in the bathroom and stepping out headfirst. When it was even, I'd get a burst of energy and I'd hear a whistling sound like my life was flying down the right path. Those were things that another person could have kept from coming.

The brick count came out odd a few too many times and so I started to get the idea that the place itself was somehow against me. It wasn't a thought that occurred to me, it was something I realized I had always believed. My first real scare came when I found a brick was missing from one of the walls, low and on a corner that I hadn't noticed. I'd walk by it, or just clean the little red crumbs where the gap met the rest of the wall. It wasn't until I realized that the dirt and bits around it on the ground were from someone's foot—from climbing on it—that I paid it any attention. When I stuck my foot in it and took a step up, I saw there was another brick missing, a whole arm's reach up, near the top. I felt something slimy up there and let go, and a few white things went plop onto the ground. At first I thought they were worms—maggots—and I froze, held my breath while my brain tried to work it out. With what I have, figuring things out can take longer than it should, and it was only when I smelled my hand that I finally realized what it was. A horrible smell. Latex and come. When

91

the scent hit my nose I heard a squeal like a saxophone. A scream.

At first I thought it had come from me, but then I saw a gang of men coming down the hallway, laughing and hollering. They burst into the atrium, carrying something over their heads, and chanting *Edmund Burke*, which was the name of the building. Said it over and over, like it had a hold on them. I saw that they were just boys, but they were giving off something I didn't like. I went upstairs to the cafeteria and stood on the landing where they wouldn't notice me, and that's when I saw what they were holding. A person. A girl. And though the boys were laughing and chanting, the sound underneath it, the one getting drowned out—the scream—was hers. She was fighting and flopping around like a person on a vibrating mattress. It looked like a prank, and I could tell by how red and sweaty their faces were that they were drunk—a deep, dark kind of drunk—and the girl wasn't. Or if she was, she wasn't anymore. At first I thought they were going to throw her through one of the windows, but then they crashed through the double doors I was just trying to wipe down, and carried her up a hill.

I watched them take her into the night like that, and my first thought was that I have to do something. My second was that I couldn't, not without losing my job, or having them come at me in the same way. The third thought was big and sticky, and picked up all the other thoughts as it rolled by. The thought was:

Something in this place makes you crazy.

A moment later, the voice that brought it to me added *you probably have it too.*

I opened up the cafeteria, but after ten minutes I decided that I had to go back. That I'd done the wrong thing by ignoring them. I went and got a scraper to take with me, the only weapon I could find, a little razor to take stickers and paint off glass. It was small, the size of a playing card, but having it on me, in my pocket, got me past my fear and down the stairs. When I got there, all the kids were on the other side of the glass, standing together—four boys and a girl—and smiling. Smiling at me. Smoking and passing a pint of something between them, their teeth and eyes white but the rest of them gone grey under the shadow of the building.

I decided to leave then, left that whole part of the building unfinished, and locked up two hours earlier than I was supposed to. The next day I had my doubts that it even happened, but the condom was still in my uniform pocket, and the next week, I found one still in its package up in that missing brick. To me, it looked like a pattern, but when I was feeling like that, everything did.

The next week, one of the walls attacked someone. I was the last person to be told, and so I just came across a whole mess of caution tape and scaffolding and tarps and dust where I was supposed to be cleaning. When I called Charles, he apologized and told me to just leave that part and move on.

He told me there was gonna be a hell of a lawsuit:

"The fucking front wall's been spitting rocks the size of grapefruits, one every ten years, but no one would listen to me about it. This time a kid happened through the door at the right exact moment and took one to the noodle."

Avoiding the mess fucked with my hours, because it took a solid 2.5 off of them, but I didn't say anything. Instead I put my hand in a locker and give it five good slams. I knew at the time that it wasn't productive but it made a kind of sense. It was about my hours, but for that poor kid too, like if I felt bad pain it could somehow straighten things out for him *and* me.

When I look back I know I was acting that way because I refused to take the pills they said I needed after my hospital stay. I thought refusing them would make me stronger, that if I could get through on my own, it would be for the better. And so in that state, thinking about what the bricks and the kids and the wall meant kind of made me decide things I shouldn't have. Like that the building was alive. That it made you a part of itself or else punished you if you didn't go along.

It gave me something to do for the rest of my nights, on my smoke breaks, in the toilet bowls. Gave me something to look for when I was doing the floors, gave me cracks to see in the ceiling and little differences to notice. I was sure the school was moving. Maybe it was all marshland underneath, or a slow sinkhole or something, but there were signs of growing and shrinking, no doubt about it. The more I thought about it, the more I remembered stuff that had been one way and was now another, like a whole door that used to be under the stairwell, and the giant mirror that was right next to the south double doors that was just gone.

"What happened to that stuff?" I would ask out loud. I wanted to ask Charles but then I wasn't really sure if he was on our side or *Edmund Burke*'s. I wanted to go look for the girl in the silver shirt from all those weeks ago, but I was both scared I wouldn't be able to find her, and that I would, that I'd lose my job up there on a hot, sticky night.

One night I walked into a beam of moonlight coming down from a little round window and got trapped. I couldn't move my body or call out for help and so instead I was stuck looking at the little crossbar in the circle and kept thinking *I'm in its sights*. I only got out of it by holding my breath and closing my eyes and imagining myself down at the other end of the lobby, doing my job. I focused on the idea long and hard until, when I opened my eyes again, that's where I was, and what I was doing.

I mostly didn't think about the building during my daytime. I'd just watch TV and smoke and take walks, but more than a few times I'd catch the tail end of an idea or a memory I'd once had that could help with my theory. Memories were hard to hold onto without booze, which had the ability to open my mind like a flower, so I even thought about buying some Russian Prince. Just so I could make my brain work right—not even to get drunk—just a few ounces to grease the wheels and get things going.

I didn't give in, though, not then. I'd get into bed and sleep when I felt like that, and eventually my missing memory came to me. Spider-man dealt with this shit once. A living building. It was a museum and it tried to kill him. And a brown or a yellow guy was in it. Like a mummy or a zombie, all rotten and shit, and he controlled the museum. He made chandeliers fly around and wax cavemen chase Spider-man. In the end, a suit of armour cut Spider-man's head off. Or no—Spider-man cut the rotting guy's head off—but it grew back.

I tried to explain it to the guy at the comic shop and he said he wasn't sure which issues I meant. He said it sounded more like a *Twilight Zone* episode but I said no, it's definitely a comic. I read it as a kid, and then again at the library in the can back in '01. It was a pretty dull day so him and me went digging through the oldies and I realized it wasn't a zombie, it was Spider-man's enemy, the Lizard. We found four Spider-man comics with museums in them, but only one of them had the lizard. It wasn't the right comic, but it was close enough that I bought it. Read it at the MacDonald's nearby, and even though it wasn't the one I remember, it seemed so familiar that it made me feel better, even if it didn't tell me how to solve my problem.

I lost the comic book before I could read it twice, but I had a dream about it. About the story I thought I remembered. In it, there was a Lizard, but not the one from the comic book. This one was my Lizard—brown and sweating and covered in bandages—there just for me. I saw him in the hall at the school, upstairs near the toilets, and he had a mean hard-on sticking out of his wrappings. Was hissing and laughing and playing with himself, trying to keep it going so he could give it to me. He didn't look exactly right, or real—he looked like a guy in a costume—but I got the idea that maybe the costume was alive, growing on the guy in patches, like moss. I knew, somehow, in the story of my mind, that he was a person who had died and come back this way, in a new body that was hell to be inside. And that he hated me and everything.

"Don't come forward," I said, but of course he did.

As he came at me, I got a jolt of pain in my guts like I'd been knifed and I fell backwards over my bucket, tipped the thing over and within seconds I was soaked in mopwater.

The monster's rubber feet squeaked after me and it was then that I realized I wasn't quite dreaming, I was seeing shit. I heard the echo of my own voice spiralling down the halls and bouncing off the floors and then it was quiet. Then I saw just how dark it was outside. That it was just another night and the hall was empty.

The doctor warned me I was probably gonna see shit. He said I'd feel good for a bit and then it would be like detox all over again. And it would be bad. I thought it had come and gone but there it was after all. At first I thought about the building, and imagined that it was using my own bad thoughts like a magnifying glass on an ant, narrowing them and making them come down on me hotter and stronger than they were in my head. But after that, when I had a drink from the fountain and a cigarette and sat down outside, I knew I would have to get those pills he talked about.

I barely finished my cleaning that night because I was so fucked up over my lizard. I kept looking over my shoulder and even fell down the stairs because of it. Ended up scraping my hands and bashing my knees and it took everything, everything in me not to walk to Ron's or whatever bar would let me in at eight a.m. to drink my face off.

It hurt to go to the doctor. To say that I fucked up and I couldn't straighten myself out on my own. But he was nice about it. He said what he said before, that it's not an option to go without the pills. That a guy as young as me can still make it if we get on top of it. He prescribed the stuff, which is usually for old people, but said it would help me keep my head sorted. He also gave me a chart of stuff to eat, vitamins to take. Said that people who have alcohol dementia need nutrition more than anything else. It's important to eat three meals, make them healthy, and never miss them.

I realized too, that I hadn't been drinking enough water, just a few cups of coffee and a can of coke to stay up. The doctor straightened all that up though, and after a while, I actually felt good. I started getting that high all the time and for a while the job got better. With something as easy as the right food the right amount of times, the right pill at the right hour, things made more sense. Three weeks is all it took for me to feel like a teenager again. At night, the school was quiet, like a church, and when I was cleaning, it was like a whole new place to me. It was like I'd just come back from another planet. One that looked just like this one if it didn't have straight lines and right angles. I stopped seeing shit, hearing shit, thinking insane thoughts, and more than once I had a hard time remembering what it was even like before the pills.

It stayed away from me, and I didn't even think about the building growing or moving, or controlling people's minds. I just about forgot all about it until I found that comic book in a bag with a bunch of porno magazines and old burger wrappers. I laughed out loud, and remembered how crazy I was being, like it was so far away from where I was. But then, I looked inside, looked a little *too* close at one of the pages. That lizard was smiling too hard, his mouth *too* wide. And I felt it, like it was fresh. I closed the book. Threw it out.

Then one night the professors get me in their office.

I'm going by with the dust mop and one of them shouts *hey* and I stop. I don't know why I stop. One of the professors has a sixty-ouncer, is drinking right out of the neck with one hand like the kids would do, except it's a fancy Scotch I've never heard of. I get the sense from looking at them that maybe something had gone wrong for one of them, and maybe the other was the kind of person who'd go along with anything.

I resist the urge to step inside, so I just stay at the doorway and they ask me questions. Nothing important. Where I grew up (In town). How long I've been a cleaner (Just for a bit). If I want a drink (No, I can't).

But they pass it back and forth to each other, and at some point, start passing it to me to give to the other guy. After a couple of passes, I watch my hand bring it to my mouth. Feel my mouth open, my throat take it and send it down to my belly, and feel everything get dull. Even though I stand there and joke with them and listen to their shit, it takes everything to keep it together. I feel like I'm falling backwards into something like a bed, but warmer. Something like water, but softer. I realize that I believe the building is moving again. I believed it with my first sip. And what's more, I've always believed it.

I want to say something like *no sorry I have to keep working*, say it now and launch it back ten minutes ago, when I was still safe outside their door frame, but I can't. I realize that going to meetings and all that probably would have trained me to say it from the get-go. I would have said it when I met them, would have shaken their hands and told them about my disorder or disease or whatever they would have instructed me to call it.

Then we're outside, and I'm on my hands and knees, showing them the slope in the ground made by the building as it moves forward.

"That's amazing," one of them says.

"This place is fucking haunted to shit anyway," the one with the beard says. "All I hear is people saying they wish the department was somewhere else. Jane saw a ghost here once."

"Fuck Jane," the other one says, then the bottle goes around again and we're leaving to get more and I don't even think about my dust mop up against the wall on the third floor. Don't think about the unlocked maintenance room, the extension cord running down an entire hallway into a stairwell. The six dirty washrooms that need to be cleaned.

We're at a bar after that, and they get us each a pitcher and we're in a place that doesn't even care if we drink right out of the jug. Then I realize we're at Ron's, and I brought us here. Nick's behind the bar, watching me, and I get the sense that maybe I'm dreaming, maybe I've floated here in a dream and really I'm in bed, groaning and rolling around and kicking the shit out of the sheets. Maybe I'm still good, and I haven't drank a drop, haven't done what I've done, and everything's okay.

"I need to put together a resume," I tell the professors. "I need to get a new job."

"Take out an ad," the younger one says, "I'm sure you can do a lot of jobs."

"I'm alive," I tell them, "got two legs. I can work."

"Is Alive and Can Move," the other one says, moving his hands like he's creating a headline before our eyes.

Then there's a long, black piece in my memory like a blindfold and then I'm on a beach with my shirt off.

"Look at that," one of the girls says. There are girls.

We look out across the harbour at the city and, even though it's late, the lights and the fog and the sky all around it are this deep purple, green, and brown at the edges like a bruise. There are clouds over top of it that aren't over us, and you can see the little flashes of lightning way in the air as things get ready to open up.

"The school's moving," I tell the professors. "In the past two months, it's moved two feet. That's why the wall almost collapsed."

"Of course it is," one of them says. "According to my research, the whole city's on the move. It wants to get into the Atlantic."

"Really?"

"It's a living thing, the city. I know that sounds like a joke, but it grows and changes and learns. Does stuff. Just like us. Except it runs on people."

"That's bullshit," I say, but I can feel myself getting scared. "Gonna need a new job."

"He's a professor," one of the girls says in a voice I don't like. Everyone looks at me like they're serious, though. Like I'm not being fucked with.

"Your body runs on a bunch of smaller things going around and doing shit. Your blood, your cells, antibodies, bacteria, all that stuff. A city's the same thing, except we're those little guys making it work, keeping it alive. You see?"

"Yeah," I tell them. And I do. I can actually see it in my mind, all of us climbing over scaffolding and driving our cars and walking up and down the streets like water through a pipe. I want to ask them if they know somewhere I can get a job, but then someone passes me a drink and I realize I don't know anyone's name, don't even know who or what they are.

"The city's gonna dump us all into the ocean," the bitchy girl says. "You think two feet is impressive? Try a kilometre a year. That's how fast the city is trying to kill us."

"It's true," the professor says, but this time I can hear something in his voice. Then his friend speaks up and I realize they've been bullshitting me, going around in circles making shit up.

Smoke pours out of the other professor's bearded mouth as thick as taffy, and he says, "Oh yeah, the world's coming to an end. This is fucking it."

Then there was thunder, and that feeling you get inside, that rumble that wants you to run away like an animal on a nature documentary, and I could almost see it. That bruise colour spreading through the sky. Everything shook—and I felt it, right in the middle of me—and the city actually *moved*, moved a whole block over. Like *ka-chunk*, and there it was, settling in, nestling into place like a cat. And the thunder got louder and louder and the sky lit up again and when it was over, when the noise from the sky got quiet, almost everyone was laughing like crazy. I could feel something coming, something coming right up from inside of me, so I make a point to try and drift off to that place where everything gets dark and I can sink into myself like a stone down to the bottom of my thoughts.

Three years later I go back to that school and eyeball it from the corner of the steps to the big oak tree out front, and I count out the paces and put my hands flat on the earth and I swear it's taking a *goddamned* walk up the city. I'm completely dry, and I'm on my medicine, and I've been stone-cold sober since I was back on the street, but I swear it's moved. It's a cold fall day and I know it doesn't make sense, but it's all there, undeniable. And I can still see that same dark shit in all the kids, staring at me as they go by. They look at me like I'm some kind of monster dragging my belly but I know that, down low, from this angle, I can see something that they never will.

CRATER ARMS

THERE ARE TWO kinds of emptiness. The one I had, and the one I needed.

The first kind is empty because it had once been filled; because something had been there and was now absent. This emptiness has a kind of pressure, which I came to see was the expectation of something that used to come around and came no longer. The disappointment of it, which was considerable.

The other kind of empty was of the not-yet-occupied, and that was the kind I wanted. So I went looking for it in the apartment listings in the newspaper and online until I got something. Anything would do, and that's what I found. I meet with a landlord. He's an enormous person, the fat on his body parcelled into segments like an insect. He has huge, pointed tits.

It's three hundred dollars a month, which is the cheapest one-bedroom I've ever heard of in this city. The cash is on me, in my shoes, and I tell the landlord I need to use the bathroom so I can get it. I close the door, take out the money, and flush the toilet before I head back out. Everything smells like boiled eggs and it's cold. I put the wad in the landlord's hand.

You make up your mind in there, huh? He asks.

Yeah, I tell him. Nice bathroom.

It needs some good hard work but it's a good deal, he says.

That it is, I say, knowing immediately he's the one who wrote the description on Kijiji. In it, *good* described the room, the building, the courtyard, and the balcony.

He stands around for a minute, looking at the money. He didn't ask for a specific amount, didn't mention anything about a deposit. No paperwork of any kind has been filled out. He pockets the money instead of counting it, scratches his swollen chin and clears his throat. Looks at me.

You—what's your name again?

I'm Rick.

I expect him to tell me his name but he doesn't. He doesn't do anything except make for the door, the floor shuddering underneath him. I think he's gone at first, but later I see him in the hallway, smoking a cigarette near an open window, January air rolling in. On the floor next to him is a bloated stack of newspapers and magazines. He's reading an Auto Trader with one hand, and there's a red New Testament facedown in his lap.

I move in.

My door is too wide for the doorway, but also too short. The floor is half that kind of zigzag woodblock flooring and half linoleum with no clear division between them. The bedroom is on a down slope and it's small, almost too small for my bed. Two pipes stick out of the wall and there's one coming up from the carpet, sealed up with hard, yellow foam. There's a crack in the bathroom wall so big I can see the back of the fridge one room over.

The view from the window is mostly of the wrought-iron sign for the building: CARTER ARMS, and beyond that, the elementary school across the street. Already, I can hear something in the walls. Already, I know it's a rat.

I find the balcony. There's a loose section of fake wood panelling leaned over the glass sliding door. Only after I try to get outside do I notice that there's a hand-written note that was stuck on the glass, now fallen onto the floor:

DO NOT GO ON BALCONY

I get the door open with a screwdriver and go out. It's cemented into the building just fine, but the railing is loose as hell. I stand in the cold and smoke a pipe. I do this every day. I don't work. I don't do anything else. I spend nearly every hour in my apartment, lying down and looking up at the lights. Trying not to think about my mother or father, or what my friends are up to. Or sometimes I'm in the hallway, reading something from the landlord's pile. Other times I wade through slush and sit on the picnic tables in the courtyard and look at the building. It's there that Serge from 204 comes out to meet me and I'm told things about the building, whether I want to hear them or not, whether I acknowledge his existence or not. Our conversation is an explanation of the world around us that could stop and start and pick up where it left off. A looped recording at a historic site in a toque and scarf, following me around:

Carter Arms was built in the forties, and has never been up to code because of war shortages. My apartment actually used to be the electrical and storage room. My bedroom was a bathroom, and my bathroom was a closet.

The landlord is just the landlord, not the owner. The owner is Mrs. Tremblay, who lives on the fourth floor, who was born in this very building. She's got some kind of muscular disorder and can't move around, so no one ever sees her.

Our floor consists of me, Serge, our landlord, our landlord's ex-wife, and a single mother and her son in 201. He says the landlord's ex-wife will sleep with me if I go there. That's all I have to do, just show up.

I nod, grunt, and say uh huh to him. Mostly I stare ahead and don't say anything, try to affect some smaller muscular disorder of my own. I hadn't counted on someone like him being here, someone trying to be pals, and I don't know how to deal with it. At night I can see the white glow of his kitchen coming through the crack in the bathroom, his fridge humming at me. Can hear him shuffling around in there, making little snapping sounds. His fingers or gum. Or maybe a fly swatter.

One night, after a long soak in the tub, I realize they're cards. He's playing solitaire.

One day, a kid on the stairs asks me why I'm living here.

The second floor? I ask.

Crater Arms. You white but you ain't old. We got white guys but they all old.

Crater Arms?

The building, stupid.

Yeah, right, I say, then try to make my way past him.

So why? He shouts down at me. Two more stairways down he shouts it again, and when I go out the door he's hanging out the window saying hey mister hey mister. When I come back later, he's gone, but there's a note under my door that says U SUCK

DICKS. It's colder than usual so I stay in my clothes, then get in a sleeping bag and get all cocooned. I want to sleep but all I can think about is crater arms, crater arms. I see them, a pair of women's arms, plump and white with red chunks out of them. Holes, craters, golf-ball-sized pieces of her eaten away. At some point I realize they're my mother's arms and, in one of those half-dreaming moments, I say (or maybe think) *it's spread to her arms*.

The next day I try to put on clean clothes, but the rat has shit in every drawer. They're dry little turds you can just shake off, but he's shat on my underwear too, which is just too much for me. I go back to my house, take the bus there, but it's so empty and so much *the same* as it always was that I can't take it. I take Mom's picture off the wall, but it leaves behind a weird kind of space so I put it back and go home to Crater Arms in my father's Acura.

I catch the landlord reading the Bible again, smoking. I don't ask to join him, but I do, taking out my pipe and lighting it. I stand while he sits and after a while he says it's funny that a young person would be smoking one of those.

I tell him my father did, but quickly change the subject.

You're religious, I say.

Yeah. Well, yeah, he coughs up and swallows some phlegm. I mean, I don't know which one is right or what have you. But there is a god, I know that.

I nod and take a few puffs.

How do you know? I ask casually.

Maybe you should talk to a minister. He looks embarrassed, clears his throat again.

I've talked to them before, I say. I want to talk to you.

After a moment or two, he takes me to 203 and knocks on the door. It opens immediately, and another fat person's there in the doorway, almost bigger than he is. She has short, curly hair and thick glasses. Introduces herself as Michelle, and invites me to come in. Her place is tidy, bigger than my room, but it's almost more empty than mine. It seems like after the separation she was the one who got the new place. The other kind of emptiness.

I'm sat between her and him, given tea and a big plate of cookies from a package. He tells her to tell me about her experience, and she gives him a look, like maybe he's out of line telling anyone about *her experience*. But she tells me about it, and only after does she think to ask if I believe in Jesus Christ. I tell her my mother did, but my father only believed in god. He said all that other stuff was a cash grab.

And what do you think, she asks.

I think you're probably telling the truth, I say.

I stare at the ceiling and think about her story for days. About the time she thought she was pregnant but when she went to the doctor it turned out she had a tumor as big as a softball. Said she didn't believe in the Bible or anything before that, but saw god the night before her surgery, standing in the corner of her room.

He'd been tall, maybe ten-feet tall, and was glowing green. He had a beard and long hair and wore green robes, but didn't speak. He came over, made her husband disappear by raising his big green eyebrows, then drove his hands into her stomach. After that, the operation yielded no results. They found zero tumors. None.

I didn't ask what that meant to her, or what she thought about all of it. I just listened. To me, it seemed much more convincing than anything I'd ever read in a bible. She said that God didn't seem like he was a spirit, it was more like he was a real thing, like he was really there in the apartment, walking around. Like if you examined the floor you'd come away with some evidence. Fibres from his robe and a footprint of crypto-zoological proportions.

I go out to buy rat traps and run into the kid again. Ask him if he's ever seen anything in the building.

Like what? he says.

Like a ghost, I say.

Yeah I saw a ghost. Had a backwards hat on and shit.

Was he green? I ask.

Hell yeah he was green. He was hella green.

I live here because my parents died, I tell him.

And they ghosts now?

Maybe, I say. I don't really know.

We stand around for a minute. He tells me his name is Jamie. I tell him mine is Rick. Do you want to go buy rat traps?

Sure, he says. We drive to Canadian Tire and buy twelve of them. Spend all afternoon setting them up, playing with them, throwing balls of paper at them and setting them off so they jump in the air. By eight o'clock, he has to go home, and there's no sign of god or the rat by then.

After a couple weeks I catch up with my best friend, the one I can't afford to keep hiding from, and the two of us go out for breakfast. There isn't really a lot for me to say, but he says a lot of what he's expected to. Am I okay, how am I doing, and how am I *really* doing? That kind of stuff. I tell him I'm doing good, and I try to explain that even though it seems like I'm doing nothing, I actually feel like I'm accomplishing something.

What *are* you doing? He asks.

If god was a real guy, I say, that would mean he lives in a real place.

That doesn't really answer anything, he says.

And so I tell him that maybe he shouldn't ask so many *dumb fucking questions* then. I say something like:

I'm doing whatever the fuck I'm doing and if I wanted you to know all about it, I'd tell you.

Then we sit around our Breakfast Slammers, not talking.

It was a cruel thing to say, and it's almost been long enough that I probably can't get away with saying things like that anymore.

In my head, we don't argue, don't part ways then and there. In my head, the way it goes is we go back to the house, and we get on top of the roof and talk about things. Not the way things are now, or even the way things used to be. We just talk about things, like movies and books, motorcycles. We would find rocks on the roof that we'd thrown up there before and have a contest throwing them as far into the woods as we could. I would get a déjà-vu feeling, or maybe a being-watched feeling.

I knock on Michelle's door, and go in. We don't have sex, but I sit there and have her read to me from the Bible until I get tired and ask her about seeing god again. She tells me her story again, and, as a bonus, tells me about a friend of a friend who was planning to kill himself by jumping off a bridge.

An eagle landed on the bridge, perched on the rail, right next to him, she says.

Eventually I ask her. If god's a real guy, could you go where he lives? And get there without having to die?

Maybe through prayer, she says.

I think if someone else had said it to me, it might've seemed like a bullshit answer. Like maybe you need to change the way your mind works, I half-ask.

She doesn't really answer, but I wasn't really asking her anyway.

In the hallway, Jamie says he heard a snap in my apartment.

We go in, and the trap near the radiator is upside down, blood sprayed on the metal.

I turn it over and there he is, at peace. One of his little pink hands is curled into a ball, the other has a couple little fingers raised.

Looks like he's asking us a question, Jamie says, and he's right. The expression on its little brown face is genuinely inquisitive, searching our huge faces for some kind of answer.

It's maybe the first nice day of spring that I wake up to an alarm. And on top of that there's a different sound—a pitter-patter kind of splattering sound. When I get dressed and go into the living room there's a narrow beam of rusty water dribbling out of the sprinkler. There's no clear indication of what's actually happening, but I get dressed anyway. I take a minute to think about what I should try to save incase there actually is a fire, and all I can think to take is the paper skeleton I'm making Jamie for science class. It doesn't have all two hundred and six bones, but it has the ones that count. It has little brass fasteners and can fold up.

Everyone's in the courtyard, looking up at the building, but it doesn't seem to be on fire. Jamie is there with his mom, clutching his Xbox. He's telling his mother he forgot his other controllers, but she says she doesn't care. She's trying to squint at the building, figure out if it's on fire or not.

And my games, he says. Then he looks at me and repeats it, so I give him the skeleton.

He looks at it, says thank you, then shows it to his mother.

Eventually the landlord comes down, out of breath. He's followed by Michelle, wheeling forward Mrs. Tremblay, who's draped in white blankets like a bride. I don't think any of us have seen her before, or at least it seems that way, because everyone's looking at her. She takes up all our focus, like she's even bigger than the apartment building.

Her skin looks smooth and soft, and her hair is long, almost down to her waist. She looks tired, her head tilted to one side like it's heavy. But she's beautiful. She's the most beautiful thing I've seen in maybe my whole life. I realize I'm surprised that something like her was here, all along, just a few flights of stairs separating her and me.

Michelle tells us it's okay, everything's going to be okay, but it sounds like it's coming from Mrs. Tremblay, speaking without moving her mouth, speaking directly into my mind.

EVERYWHERE MONEY

I QUIT BECAUSE money was everywhere.

Inside my clock. In the hollow base of my bedside lamp. In a Ziploc bag sunk to the bottom the litter box. Taped between every single page of every single issue of *Motocross* magazine from 2006 to 2010. My framed and signed Hulk Hogan picture had so much cash in it that it couldn't stay up with a regular-sized nail. My iron had six thousand dollars under the heating plate, and when I plugged it in by accident, I nearly burned down the place. Cash I didn't hide ended up chewed apart by my ex's rabbit, so it all ended up inside, or attached to, or buried under something. It was like a house crawling with cockroaches or ants or some other thing that gets inside of a place and just takes over.

It was my ex, Tan, who got me the job. We came to Montreal together, with nothing but our love, a rabbit, and her connections to various fucked-up crooks and lowlifes. She joined up with people who stole credit cards. I guess regular people or the newspaper would call it a fraud ring or something. She wouldn't give me any details about it. All I knew was she got a job as a manager at a fancy club, but her *real job* was doing something equally fancy with customers' Visas. I knew it involved the point of sale computer where all the orders were rung in and paid for, and the little USB she had on her keychain alongside a bottle opener and a tiny Mr. Potato Head missing all of its removable features. I got the idea that she was doing a more sophisticated version of my job—that I was in an entry-level criminal position and she was a semi-pro just waiting to get scooped up into the big leagues.

At my work, we got seventy-five dollars for every bank account number we nabbed, plus an on-the-books ten-dollar hourly wage with MGCI Global, which logged every hour you did as if you were in an office doing cold calls for forty-five hours. On top of that, you made a percentage on however much money they yanked out with the account number you gave them. There was no way of knowing how much cash they actually would withdraw from an account once they gave the authorization, but it wasn't unusual to have an extra grand or more in my wad at the end of the week.

I was told our boss Marcel had more offices all over the city, separate cells of scammers with no connection to one another, sometimes in actual call centres, or even working from home with a little scrambler/computer thing that plugged into your phone and randomly autodialled suckers for you. This was an option offered when we took sick days.

Our little operation was in a downtown office complex between a real estate agency and a dentist. We'd go in from noon to maybe seven, and at the end of it send off an encrypted email with the account numbers. A week later the boss personally delivered all of our money from a messenger bag bloated with cash. The wads—and I'm not exaggerating here—were as big as submarine sandwiches.

It's easy work. It's the same thing as every message in your email's junk folder, every letter that has YOU HAVE ALREADY WON printed on the envelope. You tell people they won some money from a contest (which they didn't enter), then tell them they need to give you a smaller amount of cash in order to free up the larger sum. Most people didn't fall for it. Most people would laugh and hang up, or else get pissed and start swearing at you—call you human scum, whatever. But some people didn't. Some people would give us their bank account number and authorize a cash transfer that they thought was for something like forty bucks in order to get their cool million, and our company—if you could call our company a company—ate their life savings. And that was it. Easy.

I quit because of our boss, Marcel.

He was only five-foot-seven, but he must've weighed two hundred and thirty pounds and was definitely on steroids. He was thick and wide-backed and veiny—but wore leisure wear from the seventies. Turtlenecks and polo shirts with slacks up to his ribcage, big-lapelled jackets that bunched weirdly on his huge body. He supposedly ran the whole show, and was personally involved with everything and everyone from the ground level up. It seemed like he was making it easier for the police to nab him, but I guess he had his own reasons for doing it.

When he showed up to drop off our pay, he'd have a chain wrapped around his forearm with a pair of pitbulls he called Mickey Mouse and Donald Duck at the end of it. I don't even think he knew which was which, and they definitely weren't pets. When he'd come over to my apartment, he'd let them go and they'd run around, smelling and chewing on anything in sight, barking and fighting each other. I got the idea they weren't even his.

They'd always end up at my bathroom door, sniffing and growling. He'd always ask what I had in the toilet and every single time I had to tell him it was the rabbit and there'd be a moment where he looked like he didn't believe me, like I had a SWAT team waiting in there for him. Then he'd go over how much money was in the envelope and why, one Italian loafer on the coffee table, leaning over me while I tried to act like I wasn't scared shitless of him and the dogs and his huge fucking arms.

When Tan was there, he'd be almost sweet. She'd pet the dogs and give them treats that were supposed to be for her rabbit and they'd talk like they knew each other. For all I knew, he was her boss, too.

Keep it up, he'd say, and smile, then stuff the cash into the envelope and hand it to me.

When she was out of my life, he'd chuck the money and still said *keep it up*, but it never sounded encouraging—never added *or else* onto the end, but it didn't need to be. He'd look around my apartment for a bit, look at the different messes growing in different corners, then leave. I got the idea that quitting was probably not an option, but that only made me want to quit even more.

One time I forgot to put the rabbit in the bathroom when he came for a visit. Once I realized it, I rushed around the house looking for its little broken body, but I couldn't find it anywhere. I just assumed the dogs ate it whole or carried it out of there, but then the next day it came out of some incredible hiding place and hopped around like it was no big deal. It occurred to me then that hiding is all it knows how to do. Hiding and staying completely still for long periods of time, if it's required. Have you ever seen a rabbit staying still? It's amazing. The whole of its being is capable of just sort of *stopping*. It occurred to me that the whole of my being is probably suited to doing nothing, or at least nothing meaningful. When faced with a predator like Marcel, all I can do is work at the little tasks he needs done in hopes that he realizes I'm worth slightly more alive than dead.

I quit because I didn't know what to do with my money.

My first four-grand payday, I went and bought the stuff I thought I always wanted: a leather jacket and nice clothes, badass cowboy boots, one of those cool driving caps like mobsters wear. When Tan was still here, she said I looked like a sucker, and I thought she meant my fashion sense was for shit. Later, when I was on the toilet at the McDonald's on St. Catherine's and someone stuck a pistol under the stall door, I could see what she was getting at.

The gun wasn't even aimed at me, and I could've even reached over, with my pants down, and grabbed it. But I didn't. I took all of the money out of my wallet and gave it to the hand waiting patiently next to the little gun.

Les bottes aussi, he said. Et le manteau.

And I spoke enough French to know that I was going to be walking home in my socks. On the way I got some velcro shoes and a windbreaker from the Salvation Army and didn't put on anything nicer after that. Tan said she liked my new look, but said it in a way that told me she probably knew what had happened. But that was Tan. I always had the idea that she was one step ahead of me, even if she wasn't. That she knew what I was doing even if there was no possible way she could've found out.

So instead of buying clothes and nice things, I started buying really expensive food for us, as if you could eat the money, get it into you that way, consume it. All of our labels were green or light blue, and they all said *Healthy* or *Natural* or *Organic* or *Whole Wheat*. They said *Hand-Made* and *Fair Trade* and even *Good For The Planet*. Even our beer. Even our toilet paper. They had smiling people on the box and spiralling, tribal fonts, or else were completely minimalist and mostly white.

Once she left I stopped buying it, but my cupboards were still full of packages of Pure Quinoa and Organic Falafel Mix and vacuum-sealed bags of Jasmine Rice with "freshness windows". All the fresh kale and bok choy and eggplant and litchi fruit stayed in the fridge and rotted down to nothing until I just didn't open the door anymore. My freezer remained full of fresh cuts from the deli, frozen in the plastic bags they came home in.

My money piled up.

I couldn't look to the guys at work for answers on what to do with it. Eric and Teddy were doing the kind of stuff everyone says you end up doing with a lot of money, probably because they thought they had to. Booze and clubs, drugs and gambling. Women. And by women, I mean the kind that were in the back of the free newspaper, the ones you could order over the phone like a pizza.

Eric would brag about them when we were in the office, brag about all the fucked-up shit he'd get them to do. How he'd order two and get one to sleep on the floor while he had a go at the other one, then get them to switch. He'd say he was benching them, like they were his own little basketball team. They were there at every party he threw, and Rashad said he got them so high they'd stand around and let you do anything to them.

He made one of them act like a coat rack, Rashad said. And made her stay that way. Holding our coats. He made sure we were there when he got her to do it, though. That's the thing about Eric. He does it for us, not himself.

The thing about Rashad is that he's a manic-depressive college dropout. As awkward as you could get in real life, but something between a hypnotist and a used-car salesman on the phone. A good used-car salesman, I mean. He was both the best con-guy in the office, and the one who missed the most days. Made more money than all of us, but every dollar went towards his life coach and psychiatrist and gestalt therapist and personal trainer. Every now and then he'd place a call on his cell phone in the middle of the day, and leave for the rest of his shift because he was all shook up.

One time, I heard him say *I'm entering Crisis Mode, John*. Then he listened for maybe two minutes to some kind of motivational guy on the other end, got a serious look on his face, said *All right*, and hung up. That was the day he broke the record for most numbers nabbed in a single shift (a record he set three years before).

I quit after I accidentally gave a homeless guy a box of cereal with fifteen hundred dollars in it and realized it meant nothing to me after it was gone from my life.

He was this guy I always saw in the park near my house. He's such a mess that he didn't even have shoes on most of the time. Had one of those down-filled coats, blown open and leaking feathers, tear-away pants overtop of coveralls and all of it frayed and faded a filthy brown like he'd washed it in a puddle. During the day, his bags and stuff were spread out over an entire park bench and he was up and about, doing this sort of fitness routine for money. Jumping jacks, push-ups, squats with his hands held over his head. He was deaf or crazy or something and couldn't talk—just made sounds—these roars and honks while he gestured with his open hand. He was so messed up it was impossible to guess how old or young he was. Most people couldn't even look at him. Of all the homeless people we'd see on a regular basis—the young punk ones with dreadlocks and well-fed dogs, or the bag ladies in thick, long coats, or the middle-aged guys with bad attitudes who otherwise seemed perfectly capable of working—he was the one I always thought about.

I thought to give him food because I figured he wouldn't know what to do with money. When I gave him money *anyway* it turned out he did, and the next time I saw him he had on new clothes. Or clean clothes, anyway. Work pants with the crease still in them, a warm ski jacket and hat. When he saw me, he blew out his cheeks and raised his arms over his head in a body-builder's pose. Made a sound like a trumpet, like maybe this was his greatest moment.

I felt good for a while until Tanya pointed out he was still living in the park. He was clothed and fed, but the third thing you need to survive—shelter—was the one he just couldn't manage to put together.

She leaned out the window in a tailored, low-cut black thing and asked if I really thought money would change anything. I went over and looked where she was pointing. Saw him on that bench in the rain, with the box of *Ancient Grains All-Natural Granola with Real Fruit* bloated and falling apart at his feet. I wanted to explain that I only gave him money by accident, but that seemed too stupid to believe. It wasn't like he had bowls or milk or even teeth to eat cereal *with*, so I said nothing.

If you believe in this kind of stuff, why not work at a shelter or something? She asked.

She always said just because she did skeezy stuff it didn't mean I had to. It was her favorite thing to say to me. You don't *have* to do anything you don't want to. Do anything, she would say. She said it a lot my first week, when I actually wasn't sure about what I was doing, but I could see that I needed to be the same kind of thing as her or else it wouldn't work.

There's lots of soup kitchens in the city, she said, but it didn't mean anything when she said it.

I quit because there weren't people in the city that mattered to me, and I didn't matter to anyone there either.

Once Tan was gone, it was me, the rabbit, and the guy in the park. And Mom, on the other end of the phone. I took my on-the-books job with MCGI global and ran with that story for her. So she thought I was contracted to raise funds for Stop African Poverty, a charity I made up. When she'd call, I'd invent a whole list of accomplishments just for her, like getting promoted to floor supervisor, and hint towards a possible trip to Sudan with the company.

Would you take Tanya with you? She would ask, sounding excited.

And I would say something like, *It might be the place to pop the question, don't you think?*

And then she'd be happy for a while, and everything we talked about was the engagement. I'd done the same thing before by hinting about a possible grandchild in the future, by implying she'd get to meet Tan in the new year, and by flat-out lying and saying that I already had a ring and was waiting for the perfect moment.

When Tan was gone, the only sign that she had left willingly and wasn't kidnapped or murdered or sold into slavery was that all of her shoes were gone, and everything else was left behind. I was on par with her Blend-Tech blender, her yoga mat, her ten-inch dildo. Nice to have, maybe, but you can always get another one. I appreciated, at least, that she knew when to cut her losses.

Rashad was the closest thing I had to a friend in the city, and though we never did anything outside of work, he was the person I went to talk to once she was gone. I went to him because he seemed like the only one who would even listen to the things I had to say without making fun of me.

If I would have gone there when he wasn't at a low point, gone when he was at the top of his game, I could've maybe walked out of his ultra-modern death-star condo with something useful in my head. Instead all he could say to me was shit like *that's life* and *I don't know what else you were expecting*. His weight had yo-yoed again, so he was bloated and tired and sweating too much. I needed to know if he thought I should go after her or not—if I should try to get her back, or if I should just finally let her go once and for all—or do something else entirely.

When I gave him a play-by-play of the night before and how normal everything had seemed, how we'd gone swimming at the YMCA and got drinks like every Friday, he pointed out that none of it was about me. She probably didn't even leave *you*, he said. She was leaving something else. I said *Yeah*, but it hadn't even occurred to me until then.

The best piece of advice Rashad could offer was to take stock of how much of a fuckup I was.

Obviously, he said, lying on the couch, if you're here, at this point—you probably can't do anything right.

I know I can't, he said.

Yeah?

All we can do is play catch up. So she's probably better off.

And that was just the way he talked sometimes. Other times, grabbing numbers was the greatest thing you could possibly be doing in the world. Sometimes he talked about it like it was a career, like he was a stockbroker or hedge-fund analyst or something. Talked about it like I should be proud to be invited to a party put on by our murderer boss where you can fuck the waitresses carrying around platters of free cocaine.

I quit because two men came into the office to see Eric.

He was doing his thing, going back and forth between calls and talking about what he did last night. Got two hookers to wrestle in his living room while him and his buddy watched and gave a colour-commentary play-by-play. I didn't have to look at him to know it was a lie.

It was hilarious, he said.

Before he got to the end of his story, the two men, who didn't look particularly menacing—they were wearing colourful ski jackets and Adidas trackpants and jeans—started getting in Eric's space and talking quietly to him in French. We all just sat there and watched him try to play it cool, watched him call them pals and make like it was a social visit, not business. They even put up with it for a little while.

They got him while he was showing them around in the little kitchenette in our office, showing what beverages were available in the fridge and cupboards. Got him when he leaned over to show them how the water fountain worked, which was half-insult, half him stalling for time. That's when one of them punched the back of his head mid-sip, so that the metal spray-guard around the spout was driven into his mouth and gums and destroyed four or five teeth from one side of his mouth in one swift motion.

He didn't scream. He just covered his mouth with his hand, and crouched down by the water fountain while they left. Made a continuous "mmm" sound and kept his eyes shut like he could meditate them back into his head.

The invisible hand of the market, Rashad said later. Gambling debts.

And I didn't need to know who he was in debt *to*. Marcel came in not five minutes later with a big fruit basket. He didn't say a word about the blood everywhere, the brown-and-red balls of paper towel, or Eric's wrecked face. He just sat in the middle of the room and spun around in an office chair, whistling "Sweet Caroline" and eating an apple. And Eric kept his eyes on the floor and his hand in his mouth.

Rashad, who I kept looking to when the thing was happening, hadn't even lifted his head to watch. He'd kept dialling and was still dialling at the end of it. He didn't even need to call his life coach about it.

I quit after I scammed this one woman.

She was so moved by my performance that she called me a saint. By God, a hero. *You've saved us*, she said, *you've saved the whole family.*

Then she told me about her medical bills for her son, the ones she can't pay. About how he was healthy for his whole life, but then he drowned at the pool. Drowned and was saved. She told me when they dragged him out he was blue. And in my mind I saw him as being completely blue, like something from *Star Trek*. We're trained to roll with any crazy thing the targets say over the phone, to take it and run with it, and I do my job perfectly, not trying to think about her blue kid in a wheelchair, and all the things his brain and body can't do anymore. I'd heard a lot of fucked-up stories from targets—plenty of sad ones—and this one was no more meaningful than the cancer victims or abuse survivors or sweet old ladies who were so lonely they maybe didn't even care about being robbed.

It was just the image that did something to me, that fit into the right place in my head. The image and the way she said it with her down-home folksy Texas accent. I liked to think that everyone in the office had someone like her, someone who could put the perfect combinations of words together to break the spell. They just had to hear it, and it would make them realize who—and what—they were.

It synched up perfectly with the thing Rashad said, too. I could see how everything guys like us touched—even with our voices, even with a telephone—was destined to turn to shit.

I still went through the whole process with the lady, except I wrote down a bogus bank-account number, and waited until the end of the day to file it so I didn't get an immediate bounce back email. All at once I'd made up my mind, and I was leaving.

I call my mother after that, and tell her that I've got good news.

I'll be coming home soon, maybe in the next couple days.

It's been six months since Tan's left me, and two years since I've been home, but she doesn't know that.

Did you get fired? She asks.

I tell her yeah! I did!

It's a great lie. It's believable, and disappointing enough that she won't be suspicious about what I'm doing. Will ask questions *around* my job, like it's something that might explode if she mentions it.

Are you bringing your girlfriend with you?

No, I tell her. Tan died!

My mother replies:

Did she now.

I quit by loading my stuff into the elevator and pressing the up button.

Then I take a cereal box and go down the stairs. It has odds and ends and could be anywhere between fifteen hundred and maybe five thousand bucks. I have the idea that maybe *some* of it could be useful, that my mother might like having a box of money in her life for makeup or movies or her mortgage. At first I'm okay with leaving Tan's rabbit up there but then I realize there's a really good chance it could starve to death. I get the stupid thing, and it bites me twice before I get it in the cage.

I'm terrified Marcel's going to see me, that I'm going to run into him in the lobby and that will be that. That he'll know I ducked a perfectly good number grab from the Texas woman, and I'll have to answer for it. I imagine my lie, that I must have written it down wrong, and imagine him seeing all the falseness in the sentence, like dark spots on an X-ray. Then he'd pull my head off my body right there in the street like Conan the Barbarian.

But there is no Marcel when I get downstairs, no Marcel at the bank or the corner store or the bus stop. No Marcel crouched behind Canada Post mailboxes or in behind the sculptures and paintings in the art gallery windows. No Marcel behind the row of condiments at the hot dog vendors. No Marcel in the storm drains.

I do get to see my homeless guy. After I've gone past his empty bench in the park and decided I'd probably never see him again, and after I'm on the bus, heading for the subway station. I see him through the window of the bus, a tiny shape inside the reflection of my face.

He's in a stand-off with the cops, holding a huge rock over his head. There are flashing lights and four cop cars pulled onto the sidewalk, and our route is being re-directed. He's in front of a barbecue restaurant called BARBIE-Q, with a sexy looking cow on the sign. The window's smashed out and there's blood all over the sidewalk and I can hear, even over the sirens, that he's making that trumpet sound, like he's already won. It's a sound like a horn coming down a high mountain, and I can feel it vibrating in my hands, vibrating in my cereal box.

There is absolutely no way of knowing how directly connected I am to him and the blood and the rock, if my actions led him here, but it doesn't matter. I realize this is another of those things that I'll always see, like the blue kid, or Eric smiling with his wrecked mouth. Or Tan, in her one-piece bathing suit at the YMCA pool, her chin and elbows propped upon the edge, water dripping off her skin. It makes me want to get home, get into pajamas or a sweatsuit or something soft, get into the bed that I slept in when I wasn't ready to be on my own yet. Get back in there and stay there.

Everyone's laughing and pointing and talking about him when I put my cereal box down and pull that yellow cord hanging above all our heads. Before I switch buses, I line up the rabbit's cage with my homeless guy. I open the gate right in the middle of the street, and it leaps out, runs past everything. Past me and the cops and under cars and through traffic. It shoots down the pavement until it becomes nothing more than a white ball, bouncing along in the distance. It folds in on itself and disappears without a sound, like it had never been here to begin with.

THE STORY HERE

I HAVE THE End of the World dream a lot.

So often that I don't really wake up from it with a sense of relief or joy that I'm still alive like I used to do. For a long time I'd wake up and do some real soul-searching and hug my kids and cry a little on my own. Or I'd think about the details of the dream and try to match them up to all the different elements in my life, track them back to their points of origin. An unfilled bird feeder. Spare-room linens gone unwashed for two years straight. That I haven't switched from the old-style light bulbs yet.

Now I just wake up. Look at my husband. Look at the ceiling. The clock. Listen for any signs of the kids doing anything they're not supposed to be doing. I learned to think of the dream not as something that comes to me, but as something that I have. An organ that inflates when my head is on the pillow, fills up the chambers of my mind, and takes over for the last hour before my alarm goes off.

In the dream, there's no comet or atom bomb or alien invaders. No catalyst, just a mindset that we're all in. It's just the end and everyone knows it. The only thing that gives it away is how the other people are acting. Cars are clogging the streets, guys with huge crucifixes and torches and Bibles and robes are on the sidewalk, or even on my lawn, and everyone else is just going crazy, screaming or crying or pleading with the sky like something's listening up there. A lot of people on their knees.

When I was waking up three and four times a night over it, I went to a doctor. Right away he said this sort of thing was almost always related to stress, anxiety.

Depression, he said, is often coupled with some pretty bad dreams. He asked about *crises*, about *mental stressors*, deaths in the family.

Divorces, anything like that? Divorce can be as bad as death.

No, I said. Which was a lie. But also true.

A lie because yes, we were having tons of divorces (and engagements, marriages, flings, and half-romances), but true because those things didn't mean anything to us anymore. Dad and Mom got divorced from each other twice, then proceeded to marry and divorce other people for the next two decades. Only Mom stopped trying at some point. Dad gave it another go and got a third wife. Then a fourth.

One Christmas my brother Francis and I made a chart of all my father's marriages, known and assumed infidelities, steady girlfriends, and one-offs. Frank even drew a lovechild off to the side, a little goblin baby with a line pointing to one of the girlfriends that Dad may or may not have gotten pregnant. A question mark on its forehead and in her belly. We put it all together as a diagram on a whiteboard in the basement, and even made a timeline, colour-coded it:

1. Dad and Mom marry in '75, get divorced in '93. Three kids; me and my brothers Francis and Allan. We draw pictures of us (and them).

2. From '93 to '94, Dad dates one of his students (who we weren't ever allowed to meet). I like to imagine she's a mature student returned to school after some other career, but she definitely wasn't. She was a *capital-S* Student. A kid that liked Dad's history lectures. Frank claims to have spied her and Dad eating ice cream (using Mom's bird-watching binoculars) at the park across the street.

3. Dad dates his colleague Carol from '95 to '97. Carol is well over 200 pounds and has severe physical disabilities. Teaches philosophy at the college with the aid of a microphone hooked up to a massive sound system. Is unhappy about her disability, and highly vocal about it. There was a theory going around Dad was with her to efface all prior hound-doggery. A person he can point to and say *I loved her for her mind, goddamnit.* Dad makes all of us (including Mom) go to Christmas dinner at her wheelchair-accessible place where he announces their engagement, two weeks before my wedding. Carol doesn't let us have seconds. We see her put the leftovers into Tupperware, and then into the fridge.

4. Spring 1998 Dad marries and divorces Carol. Or it might have been an annulment, I'm not sure. A ramp, half-built, remains on one side of the house like a broken waterslide. Our little brother Allan smokes cigarettes on it, dangles his legs over the edge.

5. Dad and Mom reconcile spring 1998; remarry fall 1998. Frank and I place bets on how long they have. We call it *The Sequel*. They decide this time they won't fight. They just won't. Mom smiled and told me: When we feel like fighting, we take a walk, or else go for a long drive.

6. Dad and Mom divorce Christmas 2000 within days of my first child being born. Frank wins an easy twenty bucks.

7. Dad marries a former mistress named Seline in '03. Seline is a close friend to the student we weren't allowed to meet. Her and Dad supposedly ran hot and cold during a ten-year period with brief encounters throughout. Her engagement ring is Big Carol's, banged down to almost nothing. Seline dedicates herself to becoming my best friend. Seline is a year younger than me. Seline babysits my oldest and newborn on and off, and though at first I can't stand her I come to tolerate her because I really need the help.

8. Our mother marries her probably gay best friend Marcus in '05. Marcus teaches poetry at the same university as Dad. Dad and Seline manage to finagle their way into being best man and maid-of-honour. My brother and I get astoundingly drunk at the wedding. Our little brother has dropped out of college and is somewhere in Mongolia during this time. He sends them a bone with Ghengis Khan's face carved into it as a wedding gift.

9. Mom and Marcus get divorced that same year. In '06 he moves in with her and they become *roommates, nothing more*. Marcus seems gayer than ever.

10. Dad divorces Seline the same year as if to one-up Mom. Seline is kicked out of the house and Dad immediately starts dating his fourth wife, Ronette. Ronette is the owner of a business called Clean Sweep, which specializes in the post-mortem or post-divorce removal of a loved-one's (or not-so-loved) stuff. After Seline is ejected from the house, Ronette transforms the house from Boho Chic to Pyrex-and-Doily in two weeks flat.

The chart was just something we were doing to be jerks, for a laugh. We ended up forgetting about it, and never even wiped it off when Christmas was over. When Allan took that room as his own, Francis said the whiteboard was still there, over his desk. There were a few smudges and a layer of dust, but our diagram was there, suspended over his books and homework and out in the open for everyone to see. Frank said it was untouched except for a new section that Allan had added. Documenting all the newest developments.

This is how our family works.

I am prescribed Valium.

Two weeks after I start my treatment, Dad tells us he needs to hunker down at our place while his latest divorce blows over. Even though the pills are making everything kind of dull and blurry, I know I would feel the same way regardless. It's not a surprise, and I don't care.

Of course, he doesn't actually ask to stay with us, and doesn't tell us in person, either. When my husband, two kids, and I are coming home from the movies, we find a note taped to the door, and I know what it is right away. Writing notes is my father's primary mode of communication. He left my mother with a note, moved away from us with a note, even gave me one instead of showing up at my wedding. I imagine Ronette got a note.

We stand at the front door, by the magnolias, and read it:

I left Ronette. I "need" to stay here for a while. I'm at the grocery store.

Dr. Benjamin Chesterfield.

Dad puts quotation marks around words for emphasis. He's always done this, despite a lifetime of writing papers and journal articles. When my husband reads it out loud, he says *need* like it's urgent, like Dad's dying of thirst or starvation and we're his only hope.

It means he has nowhere else to go, I tell him.

Probably, he says. He says it with all the disdain I would have for Dr. Benjamin Chesterfield if Dr. Benjamin Chesterfield weren't my father. If I were outside myself, I know I would say it exactly the same way with the exact same look on my face.

My youngest, Emma, doesn't have the wherewithal to know what's going on, but Kelly, she *knows* something is happening.

Who is that? She asks, reaching for the note.

I don't let her have it, but she's probably read it. She's an astoundingly good reader already. She probably read it backwards through the wrong side of the paper. She's like that.

It's your grandpa, I tell her.

If she can hide or control her emotions, she isn't any good at it yet. She instantly lowers her head and says *no*, like he isn't coming, like we're playing a prank on her.

Mike looks at me, like I'm the one who's done something wrong. I can't tell him to put Kelly to bed because
she's too old and it isn't bedtime yet. I tell him to put
Emma to bed instead, and Michael just looks at me, trying to figure out how to keep me from picking up my
father. One time he said he didn't like us being around
him. Us, as a couple.

I'm worried we're going to catch divorce, he said.

The other dream I have is the rockslide dream.

It's a little more inconsistent than the End of the
World one. Sometimes I'm in the house when everything collapses, when the house itself slides down the
embankment behind our yard, and I can watch everything go by out the side window like I'm on a country
drive. Other times I see the house from a distance and it
looks like a scale model—like a bad special effect from
a 1950s movie—a tiny household tumbling down with a
sea of Styrofoam rocks. One time a man with a clipboard
showed up in the dream and asked me if I was interested
in having our house destroyed. My mouth didn't move
right and I couldn't give him a straight answer, so he
checked a couple of boxes and leaned in and said he'd just
go ahead with it anyway. He walked away from the front
steps and made a hand gesture to someone or something
and that same THX-quality rumbling started up.

In the End of the World dream, it's just a normal day,
except we're all going to die and there's not one thing I
can do to stop it. I'm usually cooking our last meal ever,
or going to sleep with everyone—all of us in one big bed
like a medieval family. But the landslide one is different
because I'm not really me. I'm someone who looks like
me, and talks like me—but I'm someone else. I know

this because when I move in the dream and when I make decisions in the dream, all my actions and thoughts are so full of purpose that they're almost heroic. I grab and carry the kids in my hands like they're a couple bags of groceries, try to get them out the door and to safety.

The other difference between these dreams is that when I wake up from the end of the world, it's over. But the rockslide dream is always followed by the actual, louder-than-you'd-even-think sound of rock blasting, or stranger, more disorganized sounds of heavy machinery eating the earth. My husband is a civil engineer and can identify each of their sources. He'll roll out of bed and tilt his head towards the window, where it sounds like a choir of air-raid sirens is rehearsing, and say something like:

Industrial vacuums. That's all.

Michael's body language tells me he truly believes he's being reassuring, as if naming a sound negates how deafening and awful it is. I tell him, with my head still under the pillow:

Yes, just hearing loss. That's all.

When I complain about any of it, he makes a careful assessment before speaking. He is sympathetic about noise complaints, and about the loss of nearby wilderness where only months before we used to take the kids for walks, but only to a point. He sees himself as a champion of logic and reason, and can tolerate very little sentimentality from anyone. He said to me—when things really got rolling and I was horrified by the dry, bare earth that was left behind after the forest floor was ripped out like an old carpet—that I was wrong:

It was the same way here, right here, he said, pointing at our kitchen floor. Three years ago, this looked like that, but they developed it for us and now they're doing the same thing, right there, for other people who aren't here yet. But will be.

Yeah, I know, I tell him, I know, but it still really sucks, doesn't it?

He doesn't answer. Inside him, there is no instrument to measure this sort of thing.

The neighbourhood really does sit up on an embankment, and all of our backyards really do run right to the edge of a steep cliff. But a rockslide really is impossible, Michael insists. He goes back to the numbers, back to the physics and the geology. When our neighbours talk of cracked foundations from drilling, of eroding lawns, or, god forbid, a large-scale collapse of some kind, all their fear is met with a passionate resistance bordering on fervour. Said, over the fence to our neighbour, Mr. Fry, who claims his lawn is sinking:

You'd need three-digit amplitudes for any of that sort of thing, and we just aren't damn well getting that much, Gord. It is simply impossible.

Said to Mrs. Fry (who claimed a basement wall has begun to bulge, ever so slightly), in a tone just below a shout:

There is no dynamic amplification response in below-ground structures, regardless of vibration.

Said to me, after I mention the word "rock-slide" for a second time in one day:

That's about as likely as if we turn on our taps and snakes come out instead of water, Margie. Do you understand? Rock failure does not work like that.

Despite all of this, when the first blast occurred, and both of us jumped out of bed and didn't know what to do for a moment, he had a look on his face like I've never seen before, that something beyond his comprehension was taking place. An indignant fury under that shallow panic, one that came back to us when we found the letter from the developer in our mailbox. Despite the warmth of the logo with the family and dog standing together, the sun shining behind them, the letter is little more than an afterthought:

ATTN: Residents

Please be advised that blasting for the new subdivision commences today. It may be very loud. We apologize for the inconvenience.

I see Dad's RV in the parking lot, his cat Suzanne—who was given the title *The Only Woman Ben Never Left* by Frank and me—in the passenger seat. Of course, the first Suzanne, the one we grew up with, is dead. This one is Suzanne II, but she's at least twenty years old, if not more.

Dad's in the grocery store, having a Coke and a snack in the little café tacked onto the side of it. When I see him, I can tell he's been on the road for days just by how oily his skin is. He's wearing shorts and sandals, a t-shirt that can barely contain his gut. It would be impossible to guess from the warped WEST COAST CHOPPER logo on his chest and the big sandwich he's plowing through, that he's a tenured professor of military history. There was a time when he looked like George Clooney with a big beard, but to see him here like this—on the too-small-for-him wrought-iron chair—is like looking at a different person.

Most of our memories aren't fair, and don't necessarily show us anything meaningful or true about the person we're thinking of. They're usually just a few moments that we just can't get rid of. For me, Dad will always be Young Dad, with a navy beard and a big smile. Dad with me in his arms, his body nice and cool against mine. Kissing my head and neck and face and carrying me down the stairs saying *let's get away from those gross boys.* Him putting on his *Beach Boys*-style captain's hat and taking me out in his professor buddy's little motorboat—the one he was allowed to take out when the guy was on vacation—saying that it was our secret. The three of us burning across the harbour, him with a cigar in his teeth, the first Suzanne curled into a terrified ball, and me holding his can of Guinness between my knees so the coast guard wouldn't see.

And likewise, even though she's always smiling, my mom will always be Sad Mom to me.

Sad Mom is usually crying in the garage, sitting on the deep-freeze and screaming for me to *leave her the hell alone.* Me gazing up her dress, at her big, smooth legs and white panties with black pubic hair darkening out the front. *Good girls don't do that,* she'd said, which was harmless, and probably the only right thing to say in that situation. But it still hurt, and still made my stomach clench and sink. Still made me cry and hate her and punch and kick when she tried to pick me up and take me to my room.

It's so easy to hate Dad. So easy because he doesn't say much, and when he does, it's something that hurts or wrecks the delicate balance of things. Even easier now that he's ugly. Simple to point at the women strewn all around him and say *BAD.* But it isn't fair. And it doesn't mean anything when you hold it up to the memory of him in that sailor's hat, or the feeling of his beard against your neck, or the sound of his voice rattling down your spine saying *I love you forever Margie.*

This is something I try to convey to Michael in the same way he tries to explain things like structural dynamics to me.

At the grocery, Dad doesn't bother to explain why his latest marriage is over. The way he looks, I know he doesn't want to talk about it.

I just want to park in the driveway, he says. I don't need to stay with you.

No, I tell him, and the next thing I know I'm doing what my brothers and husband always accuse me of. Falling all over myself to accommodate him:

You can have our bed, I say. We can sleep on the couch while you're here. I know how uncomfortable that camper is.

No, he says. I should be in the camper. I just need to hook up to your hose, that's all.

He tells me he's going to stay for maybe a week. He's going East, going on the road for his leave of absence, and that he thought he ought to see me before he disappears.

Disappear, I laugh. What, are you never coming back?

No. But I don't know where I'm going or how long I'll be.

He looks off at the parked cars.

Don't know, he says again. Finishes his sandwich and is nearly out of breath by the end. When his belly rises it gets so big he looks like he's in his third trimester.

Frank and I added a little algorithm to our infidelity timeline, off to the side. It was for how much weight he puts on per woman, and how much shittier he acts as a result. He'd been a smiling, charismatic person once. Once, he could've been a game-show host or a politician or a movie star. His students loved his classes, and Mom's ex, Marcus, said his courses were always filled earlier than anyone else's, just because people liked him. He had this smile. All the lines are still there on his face—ready to go—but at some point it just stopped showing up.

When we get home, Michael gets mad at me for insisting that Dad sleep inside the house. For trying to give him our bed.

What's wrong with his *Shaggin' Wagon*?

He can't decide if he wants to start a fight about it or not, so it's all just jokes for now. It's halfway sweet that he feels the need to protect me from my own father. And halfway insulting. I get mad at him for getting mad and pretending he's not. I do it by pretending I'm not.

But Dad saves face by claiming the couch as his own. He gets his own pillows from the RV. They're brown and musty and have probably never been washed. Then he pushes his shape and smell into the cushions for a week and a half. He and Michael exchange a maximum of sixty words a day. They are both alike and unalike, and give each other a wide berth, aware of each other and their respective positions. They occupy the same physical space, but at different times. You see this stuff in nature documentaries.

The only good that comes of it is that my dreams stop for a while, though I don't know if it's him or the Valium. If it's him, I don't understand it at all. It isn't like I feel any safer or reassured having him around. It isn't like his presence calms anybody down. But the dreams stop nonetheless, and I feel okay when I wake up. I even have a nice dream for once. Something crazy and silly that I barely remember. A baby elephant thing, running around on the beach. Allan is in it, maybe. I don't know if it means anything, but at least nobody dies.

One morning I creep downstairs and he's still asleep—so I watch him. I try to see if his big body is giving off beams or waves or particles that calm you down, but I don't notice anything. Nothing happens.

Later, Dad's newest ex, Ronette, shows up.

She comes right up to the door and bangs on it with all of her gold rings, her wrinkled head blurry but unmistakable through the frosted glass. I shoot a look at Michael, and paralyze him in the kitchen like a buck in headlights so I can answer the door first. I can see how he might leverage her presence into an argument about why Dad shouldn't be here.

And Dad, he sees her through the window and right away drops his *National Geographic*. His cat runs out of the room and he makes a little sound like he's got cramps.

I open up the door and she looks past me. Searches my house over my shoulder.

Is Benny in there? Ronette asks in a crazy voice. Tell him I got his note.

Her make-up looks like it was put on in an earthquake, or else washed away in a flood.

No, I tell her. He isn't here.

Then what's the camper doing here?!

She screams it—really screams—with her hands curled into claws and everything. It makes it easier to lie to her, and I even come up with something halfway believable.

He dropped it off on his way past. Says he doesn't need it anymore.

Yes he does, she says, shaking her head, her face working itself towards collapse. Then she half-screams the word *camping*, like it's a swearword.

He's not here, I say.

He's leaving me, she says, then sort of jolts like she's in pain and I get the idea that it's the first time she's said it out loud. There's a look on her face like she's realizing it— really thinking about what it means—and I watch her body react. It moves through her like a chill. What Ben's mother would have said was *a goose on your grave.* Then she's crying and trying to open the screen door, but it's locked.

You're having a fucking family reunion, she hisses.

It's locked, I say.

I just—

It's locked, I say again. He was here, now he's gone. I'm not inviting you in.

She tries opening the screen door with one last jerk, so I close the main one instead. Lock that too, and then she's knocking again, sobbing and moaning on the other side of it.

Is that Grandma? Emma asks from behind me.

I turn around and see that Michael has both hands on her shoulders. They're standing in the kitchen watching me. No.

I think about how this will look to them when it's a memory recalled, years later. I turn and speak with my back to them so she only hears the lie, doesn't see it actually come out of my mouth:

That's not Grandma.

I don't want her to look out the window and see that it *is* the grandma she grew up with. Don't want her to know that you can go from being somebody to nobody just like that.

145

Or at least not yet. We can probably make it six years before she learns that.

I end up standing with my back to the door while Ronette pounds away, like I can shield her from it.

It's a neighbour, I tell her. Mrs. Fry.

But then Dad speaks up and ruins the rest of it. His voice shoots up at us, a booming, commanding noise from some place we can't locate. I look around until I see that he's crawled between the couch and the armchair, to a little crack the girls get into. He takes the whole space up with his body, like he's a new piece of furniture. A blanket is wrapped around his shoulders and he looks like he's all head. Like some Indian god on a totem pole.

No, he says. Says it extra loud so Ronette can hear through all the wood and glass separating us.

No. That's not Grandma anymore.

Then he looks up at me, and so do Emma and Michael, because everyone's waiting to see what I do. But I do nothing. I do the same thing as each of them and try to ignore the woman on our lawn and move forward into the completely ordinary day we're supposed to be having.

Ronette's visit is the only time his voice booms through our house. After that it's just a muffle, just a few things here and there, about how good my cooking is, or tiny little questions and comments for the girls. Teaching them about the different tracks running through the backyard, telling them about how raccoon families work. Crouching beside them while they walk their Barbies around the house, asking them what the story is. That's one of his little sayings, one that's worked its

way into all of us. *What's the story here?* Even my brother
Frank says it when I call him a few days into Dad's visit.
Says it when I tell him that I've got a visitor.

Well, he says. What's the story there?

He's going to disappear, I guess.

Where? Frank asks. He's excited, always excited to
hear news about Dad. He treats all of it like some crazy
joke he's hearing about other people—people who
aren't us. Like a TV show he used to watch, but lost
track of.

He's on some trip across the country.

Oh man, he says. I knew it. You'll never guess who
else is.

Who?

The Boy Wonder, he laughs. He means our little
brother, Allan.

Really?

Swear to god. Except he's going the other way.
They'll probably meet in the middle.

I see it in my mind like one of those dumb road-trip
movies, a father and son reconnecting. Arguing, laughing, crying. Maybe around a campfire. The car's broken
down. They drink Jack Daniel's. Argue about the radio.
Born to be Wild playing in the background. Critics call
My Old Man the most heart-warming movie since *Juno*.

Then Frank tells me he's coming over. Says it fast,
like he's in a hurry, and says he'll be over by supper. I tell
him I don't need more company here and he says it'll
be fine and hangs up, which means now I'm going to
have to make dinner for all of us, and make something
good since it's now officially a family gathering. I tell
Michael that my brother's coming over for dinner and
he knows instinctively to come over and give me a big

147

hug and kiss. I'm not done being mad at him and I kind of hate that I need him to do this, but it makes me feel like we're at least on the same team again.

Hey, he says to the girls. Your Uncle Frank's coming over.

They're watching TV, some cartoon with a fuzzy blue thing that keeps rolling around on the ground. The both of them don't bother to look up.

No, Kelly says in that shitty voice. Says it without looking up.

I tell her she needs to stop saying that, and she rolls her eyes. The other one blows air out her mouth, sticks her tongue out and makes a cuckoo gesture at her temple. Starts laughing until she falls over. Starts rolling around like the thing on the screen.

I tell them to get in the car. We're going to get groceries.

I can go, Michael says. What do we need?

No, we're all going, I tell him.

It's good to get out of the house.

What about Grandpa? Kelly asks.

I look around, and realize I don't even know where he is. Last I saw him he was in a lawn chair, smoking cigarettes and putting his butts into the birdbath. On an unnatural-looking dip in the ground, the spot I'd been asking Michael about for weeks now, because it looks like it might be a sinkhole.

He stays where he is, I say.

My memories are all tied up to that house we grew up in, the one that Allan still lives in now. I almost think of it as the place where my memories are stored, like you could look in Frank's room and it's all movie trivia, and then go down to the basement and see all the stuff I was forced to remember in my MA program packed into the soggy boxes by the water heater. All my ex-boyfriends shirtless and lying underneath the pink insulation of the attic like a duvet.

I can't imagine what it must be like to live there, but then I can't imagine what it would be like to be Allan at all. To be trailing behind me and Frank while we laugh at something that really isn't funny, to have to grow up in our family with no one but Mom on his side. Even though I call him every month and ask all the things I'm supposed to ask, there are a lot of silences, and a lot of long-distance minutes eaten up by his quiet yawns and short *mm-hmms*. There's a lot of him saying outrageous things that I don't know how to take:

I'm going to take up skydiving. I am going to dive in the sky.

I remember the day I told them about what it's like to go out on the boat—told them that it was *our* boat, even though it wasn't—and the look it brought forth on Allan's face. He couldn't believe Dad had something so incredible that he wasn't sharing with everyone. Not even a secret, just something that he had never bothered to include us in. And Frank just laughed, said *of course*, which I think meant he both did and *didn't* believe, or maybe believed it and wished he didn't. Frank has always possessed the ability to go outside of his own body, even if only to laugh at himself.

I remember that day most because it was the day Frank took the globe out of Dad's study. He wrenched it out of its stand and opened it up at the seams. It was old—not an antique, but an expensive replica of one—and showed routes for the British Royal Navy. We had spent the entire day picking handfuls and handfuls of those red berries that covered all the trees around the house—*puke berries, cause they make you puke*—without knowing why, but knowing it would be good. When we turned in our harvest, he told us it was so he could fill the globe with them, and right away Allan began to shout *NO* over and over, horrified that he was now an accessory to our crime. I told Frank I wouldn't help him either, but I stood in the doorway of the office watching him stick handful after goopy handful inside. Then, when he couldn't close the thing back up, he lied and said it didn't matter. He said to me that his plan was to throw it off the roof anyway.

When he got up there, Allan and I watched him balance on one foot, drop the globe in front of him, and boot it across the street and over the power lines like a kickball.

I wasn't aware of it at the time, but looking back I realize this kind of thing could only happen when something major was going on. He always timed it out perfectly so that whatever he did lined up with something worse: Mom's maybe-on-purpose car accident, a (female) student showing up at the house just to say hi, or the time Frank drew on Dad's picture in the paper, wrote *cheating beard* right on his face. The day I told them about the speed boat, it was a big one—Dad's crazy credit card bills for hotel rooms and champagne and room service from his trip to the island that was supposed to be about PEI's naval history and *not* about whomever he split all those lobster rolls with.

Frank was the oldest, so he always had the best idea of what was going on, what it all meant, and how to use it for his own personal gain.

And that's my permanent Frank memory; that's how he'll always look to me.

Skinny, with a shaved head, limbs growing out of his t-shirt and shorts faster than they should—holding my father's outdated planet over his head, getting ready to smash it open, getting ready for crazy reds and purples to shoot out for everyone to see.

It doesn't matter that now he has a stable, reasonable-looking woman next to him, holding his hand. Doesn't matter that he says mostly rational things and talks in a slow, steady voice. All I see is him getting ready to laugh, really laugh—laugh so hard his eyes roll back into his head and we all get worried for him.

All I can feel is what it's like to be in the middle, to be excited and scared that he'll swing back from being funny to being crazy or mean or cruel.

The next morning I find six empty bottles of wine, not counting the one that exploded on the cement out back. Two are in the kitchen. One is in the living room, on the very top of the tall cabinet where the board games are kept. One is in the big rubber tree plant pot, shoved neck-down into the soil. The last two are in the upstairs and downstairs bathroom, in the sink and garbage, respectively. Four of the bottles are commemorative wines from Dad's third wedding. Him (looking suave and dashing with salt-and-pepper hair and beard) and Seline (with thick, black hair and a tanned face with too much foundation) smiling on the labels marked *Benjamin and Seline Chesterfield 2003* in thick cursive.

I'm up before everyone, and even though my head feels like it's going to cave in, there's too much that I have to do. Too much to hide from the girls. I have to do the dishes, clear the leftovers, vacuum, mop and sweep and wipe everything down. Change the garbage and take it out.

Answer the door and tell Ronette to leave.

Put away the Pictionary game strewn across the kitchen table, try to remove Frank's sketch of a hamburger on wheels (*fast food*) stuck to the table. Get breakfast going for all of us and try to get everyone up.

Crystal is on the couch, Dad's in the camper, and Frank and Michael are asleep in our bed. I woke up in Emma's room, sleeping with the gigantic snake we won her at the fair, my arms and legs wrapped around it like a chunk of shipwreck. The girls, at least, are where they're supposed to be.

There's an idea in my head that if I make the place look better than it did last night, I can cancel out any long-term damage I may have caused them.

The only person who gets up is the one person I thought to let sleep—Frank's girlfriend, Crystal, who I probably woke up with any number of the appliances I turned on just feet away from her head. She comes towards me quietly with one of those looks on her face—something between embarrassment and understanding—like we'd shared in something we shouldn't have.

There had been a few nights like this, but just a few, and none since Emma was born. Nights where I drink enough that it feels like years are sloughing off of me, like water eroding rock. And suddenly I feel more like twenty, or even thirty. A fun number that makes it okay to say or do whatever dumb thing comes into your dumb mind at that dumb moment.

A number that lets you do things like drink enough wine that your girls laugh at everything you say and marvel at your purple mouth. That lets you show them your tongue and teeth, tell them that you've *gone purple*.

Lets you consider (only for a moment) giving the oldest one a half a glass when she says she wants to be purple, too.

Lets you tell them—in a half-assed effort to impart some wisdom—that purple ladies don't get anywhere in life (though it's okay to be purple once in a while, on special occasions).

Crystal and I have coffee and don't say much, because more and more things are rising up and bobbing on the surface. There's a conversation that we don't have, and the one that we do tiptoes around the list that stacks up between us, between our hands and coffees. The list is long. A list of things I shouldn't have done.

Last night was fun, I say.

It was funny. Mostly funny, she says.

1. Agreeing to let the girls stay up way past their bedtime, and giving into their totally nonsensical requests to wear my clothes over their pajamas.

2. Leading all of us through the backyard, the girls back with Dad. Walking barefoot and in flip-flops down the cliffside to the big hole with caution tape around it. Down to the place where the girls aren't allowed to go. Shouting things down into it. Things meant for Dad's ears, just inches away from my mouth. *Is Ronette down there?*

I'm so happy for you guys, I tell her.

I know you are.

I can't wait until the summer. It's going to be beautiful.

3. Responding to Frank's announcement that he and Crystal are engaged by interrupting mid-sentence and saying *she'll make an excellent first wife* and bursting into uncontrollable laughter right in front of everyone, including the girls. Including Dad.

It's nice that I can start to think about having a family in the next few years, she says. I almost thought it wouldn't happen.

You'll make a great mom, I can tell. And I've always thought Frank would be a really great father.

4. Allowing the girls to cut up a Barbie with wire cutters that Michael has left on the table from fixing something. Telling them that it's not a big deal because Barbie is a pretty shitty female role model anyway. Telling everyone that promiscuity already runs in our family, that we don't need to encourage it further. Realizing too late that I actually said these things out loud. Realizing a second later, and still too late, that Kelly has already sliced and diced Barbie before I could stop her. The limbs, the two hands, the feet, and the blonde, severed head resting in a pile, and me seeing and knowing that Emma, little Emma, hasn't moved on yet. Still had a few more years to go with her toys.

Crystal smiles. I don't know her well enough to know how good a liar she is.

Did you like dinner? I ask.

It was so good, she nods. It was really good.

5. Confronting Dad in front of everyone at the table for showing up, uninvited, to the house. Explaining how I

think he showed up to *my* house because I'm a woman, and he arranges the women in his life as a chain of hide-outs from other women. Explaining (while simultaneously developing terrible hiccups) that I never forgot the thing he said—sorry—*wrote* and *delivered to me* on my wedding night, on robin's-egg-blue parchment: that it's important to move forward with my education and not end up *a woman and nothing else*. That I should be a woman with goals, not just a bearer of children and a keeper of a household. Explaining (now hiccupping even worse) that since I didn't live up to his goals, I must now officially be a lesser being—relegated to the keeper of some burrow he can run to when his tail's between his legs and everything's gone wrong again.

6. Getting into a totally absurd fight with my husband and brother about nothing. My brother calling me a crazy fat lady. My brother throwing little pink body parts at me and telling me to *go cry somewhere else*.

7. Me, doing exactly what he says. Running to the bathroom with a whole bottle of *Dad and Seline '03* to hang half my body out of the window like a Muppet and drink it. Waiting for someone to come and get me, and throwing my arms around Crystal and thanking her when she shows up. Hugging her and crying and laughing all at once even when she sits on the toilet and starts to pee.

I had fun, Crystal says.

Later, everyone else is up. Frank and Michael are covered in scratches and bruises, but aren't embarrassed about it. They saw that family of raccoons march across the fence in the backyard and chased them down the hill, through the bushes and brambles. The both of them slid on flat, wet rocks and rolled down the embankment to the empty lot below. On top of whatever wine was consumed, the two of them got into a quart of Scotch whiskey that had been in the cupboard since Michael first got certified as an engineer. If nothing else, the two of them seem closer, but I decide, looking at their eyes, that they might just still be drunk.

Frank and Crystal aren't ready to drive anywhere and so they stay the rest of the morning and afternoon and the four of us watch Disney movies with the girls, four in a row, until we can finally get up and stop them from sliding another tape into the slot. From one movie to the next it dawns on us that Dad hasn't come in yet, and eventually I go out to the camper around four o'clock, after Quasimodo dies.

I can see him in the back, his belly rising and falling, hands behind his head. When I call his name, his eyes open, but he doesn't say anything, doesn't respond. I ask him if he wants dinner, or wants to say goodbye to Frank and Crystal.

I see his eyes move towards me through the screen and glass, then move back to the ceiling. They close. He clears his throat, but not to say anything to me. Closes his eyes like maybe he's trying to find his way back into a dream I shook him out of. I didn't realize until later that I was wishing or praying that the neighbourhood would drop down into itself right then and there. It only came when I sat down on the toilet to take my pills and realized I was sad that everything was still the same, even after all that.

When the noise starts, I'm out of bed instantly, and then I'm in and out of each of the girls' rooms.

Then there's more screaming and windows rattling and explosions. I'm halfway down the stairs before I realize I'm carrying both of the girls by their pajamas, my tits flopping up and down in my t-shirt. My movements are perfectly timed and in sequence: get down the stairs, drop the girls, grab the keys, open the door, grab the girls again, get to the car.

But somewhere along the way there's a voice shouting my name. Shouting MAGGIE MAGGIE WHAT ARE YOU DOING?

And another saying *whoa, whoa whoa.*

The first is my husband—naked—and the second is Frank—who has somehow dressed himself in jeans—the both of them coming down the stairs after me. There's a quick minute where I catch a glimpse of myself in the mirror by the door and everything slows down.

There is no big Hollywood rumble, no shaking, or groaning and roaring as the house separates and the mountain eats us.

Emma is crying, but Kelly is not. When I let them go, Emma runs to Michael, but Kelly stands up next to me. The fabric of my shirt is ancient, and it feels like she can see through me completely.

What are you doing, she says in the same tone as Michael.

And then there's another bang, and this time a window flashes. That's when I realize it's a gun, Dad's shotgun. The one mounted up in the camper wall by the cupboards. It's like I'm drunk again, and none of the decisions I'm making have meaning anymore. I still feel like there's something going on with the ground itself, and my first thought is that Dad is shooting the ground, that he's making real one of Michael's terms. *Using demolitions to blast slope areas* or *exerting non-static forces.* So when I open the door and go out and the girls follow me and Michael says my name again, I'm still operating under the assumption that we're all going to die anyway.

Dad's shirtless, with a smear of blood across his stomach. He's holding his gun, but something else too, trying to juggle them both. At first I think it's Suzanne, but the fur is too dark. Then I see that big, cartoonish tail, black-and-white rings when he tries to open his shotgun, and drops its broken body. I look at the fangs in its open mouth as Dad reloads.

He fires again, through the driveway and into our backyard, and this time I snap out of it, pick Emma up and hold her against me. When I take her upstairs, she's pressed against my nipple and it's like I'm feeding her again, except now she can say my name and walk around on her own. When I get up to bed, Michael's there with a sweater wrapped around his waist like a skirt without a back. He's got an expression that I saw the other night, like he's wondering if he needs me in all of this.

I focus on putting Emma to bed instead, and it's only when she asks me if I'm okay that I realize I'm not, and I try not to start crying then and there. Instead I tell her everything's okay.

Later, in Kelly's room, she tells Michael that she hates Grandpa. It's dark and I can't see him but I know that he's looking at me, or else is going to look at me and give me some kind of ultimatum. I can feel it, and I swear it's coming.

But it doesn't.

Don't say that, Michael tells her. He can't say *that's not true,* or *no you don't.* But he says she shouldn't.

That's your family, he says.

I took it for granted that Frank and Crystal would use the raccoon attack as an opportunity to finally leave.

Instead, it was decided that Frank's muscle car was the fastest way to get Suzanne to the twenty-four-hour veterinary clinic. There were two, one in the city (which didn't have room for us) and one a half-an-hour away and outside of town (which did). I was there, too, wearing clothes this time, helping Dad hold the cat on the way there, keeping pressure on the beach towel she was wrapped in while she screamed in that horrible baby voice that cats can have.

The things had torn out big pieces of her hind legs so that big chunks of meat were hanging off her, but the worst was where they had gotten under her, torn open her stomach so that all her guts came out. After shooting and killing two of the raccoons (and picking their bodies up as he went—later telling us that he knew you need to keep their heads to find out if they're rabid or not), he shoved Suzanne's bowels back into place and wrapped her up in one of those elastic sprain bandages, then swaddled her in a green-and-pink towel right there in the yard. He had deep gashes in his arms and hands from her claws and teeth, from when she was crazy with pain and trying to kill anything that came near her before they killed her. I was covered in cat blood, but he had at least three kinds on him, including his own. The raccoons were in a garbage bag in the trunk.

Frank smiled and told Dad that he probably had rabies now.

In your bloodstream, right now. Like a werewolf.

And despite the mean look on his face when he said it, Frank didn't say anything about the heavy red pools forming on his cream-coloured upholstery. Didn't say anything, though I could see his eyes darting around in the rear-view, thinking about how much it was going to cost to get it back to car-show perfect.

Then it's just Frank and me, in the waiting room, looking at a faded mural of sick cats and dogs lined up like a group mugshot, with bandages and eyepatches, thermometers in their mouths and ice packs on their heads. Nothing to read but fake magazines printed up by Pedigree foods and Whiskas. Dad had used his booming voice on the sleepy veterinarians to say he would not leave his cat's side, and so he's in there wearing one of Michael's old t-shirts (a giant one that says Sunday Fun Run and features a clown in jogging shorts) that barely fits him. He's in there like that with the pet doctor, the pet surgeon, and the helper.

You think Suzanne's gonna make it? I ask.

You think *Benjamin's* gonna make it? He raises his eyebrows.

He's always called him Benjamin, never Dad, even when he was a boy. He smiles, and my hand instinctively twitches.

Fuck you.

Come on, he says.

Did you see him? Because I did. I was sitting next to him back there.

And then he smiles again and says

You'd think he'd be used to—

But before he finishes and says whatever the rest was (used to losing women or used to relationships ending prematurely or something), I actually grab his face. I grab his smirk, right on the laugh line, where the corner of his mouth meets his cheek, and I twist, hard. He sort of moans and has to wrench his whole head backward to get it out of my hand. When he does I hear myself bark.

Why are you even here?!

Instead of answering, he just holds his hand over where his smirk used to be, and looks at me. My hand remains curled into a claw between us.

The last time this happened, the last time I wasn't on board with him and got this upset, I was sixteen. I'd put a dent in the car after my first drive and after crying for maybe an hour straight, he came up to me and said it looked like I'd been in the *Indy-Tard 500*. And I punched him in the mouth. We were roughly the same size back then, so he didn't hold back, and we had our first real fight on the olive-green carpet. I scratched and bit and tore his thin little earring out of his lobe, and he folded my nose over with his fist and left me with a funny bump that's been with me since.

This time, he sits in silence, and looks at the floor for a while, his mouth and cheeks reddening. Then he gets up, and pours us coffees from the little station by the dog-food magazines. He hands me a paper cup, and only when I take it can I see that my hand is trembling, and that his is too.

I'm sorry, he says.

He looks at me for a while. Takes a sip and sits down next to me again.

I knew he was coming.

Dad told you he was coming here?

I'm the one who told him it was okay to come stay with you in the first place. I mean, I wanted to come, so I could announce—you know—getting married and all that. And then I thought, well, maybe it could be a family reunion.

And you didn't tell me this, why?

Well, I did it wrong, he says. Boy Wonder is supposed to come, but he was already leaving on his trip. I told him we'd have a family reunion next summer.

Great, I say.

I know it didn't work, and I know now it was a bad idea, but it was supposed to be a surprise.

What makes you think I'd want a surprise?

You're right, he says. But I mean. When's the last time you saw me try to do anything like this?

I think about it. There's a deep red mark in the middle of his cheek, blooming.

I don't know.

I'm trying to be nicer.

Well, I tell him, thanks.

He rubs his face, and rotates his head. Puts his hand on his neck.

You know what Allan told me?

What?

He said when you and I left for college, Mom cheated on Benjamin.

I look at him. He stresses the key difference in his statement using his hands:

Mom cheated *on Dad*.

Then he tells me.

Allan came home one day—early, of course—and there was a man at the top of the stairs. Naked except for his head. Crouched up there, wearing Frank's motor-cycle helmet. And when he saw Allan, the guy ran and hid in my old bedroom. Locked himself in there. Allan found mom under the covers, and she made him prom-ise not to tell.

I think about it for a while. And then I ask him why he's telling me.

Allan asked me to. He said that when he saw that it changed everything for him, and that we both needed to know about it. He said it was like looking at a different person altogether. That he felt like if he took the covers off her, she'd have a Martian's body or something.

Frank, what could that *possibly* change in my life?

He looks at his reflection in the coffee for a while, trying to choose his words.

I think it's maybe that there are no good guys or bad guys in our family like we thought there were?

Then there's another long pause, and I can't decide if this is means something, or if it's just another thing he's throwing off the roof. I decide to take him seriously:

Who thought that? I've never thought that.

I know, but I thought you thought I did, he says.

I don't think like that, I tell him.

Me neither, he says, and the two of us look straight ahead at all those animals.

They want to keep Suzanne overnight, but Dad refuses, says that if she's stabilized, she needs to be home with him. They say she *isn't* stabilaized, and he says *like hell she isn't*. So he has them construct a kind of container for her body with a hole that her head sticks through. Give her one of those cones, so that she looks like a crazy household appliance. Then they send Dad home with this liquid medicine that he has to use an eyedropper to feed her with. He won't tell us how much it cost, but we saw him give them all the cash in his wallet, and then his Visa on top of that. The next day, Dad stays on the couch with his cat contraption in his lap and feeds her that brown stuff while the whole neighbourhood rattles.

Then Mom comes to visit while I'm making pancakes because Frank wasn't exaggerating, the only person who couldn't come was Allan, and this basically *is* a family reunion. Her gay-best-friend-ex-husband-poet Marcus is with her, and they're in full-blown platonic mode, their arms linked and wearing matching plaid like they're going to a barn-dance. We're having breakfast and Crystal has to pull out the table leaf and sends Frank for more chairs to accommodate them.

She has an envelope of pictures that she printed off of Allan's Facebook, and they travel around the breakfast table. They're all pretty boring, him on a Tarzan rope on some lake, him and a bunch of girls, him and his girlfriend.

When it gets to Dad, I hear a sound I haven't heard since before the girls were born. He's laughing, and it's that deep, hearty laugh. The one you'd hear coming out of his office when the dean or Marcus was visiting. The old-boys-club laugh. We all look at him but he doesn't pay attention to any of us. And even though his cat is in a bucket fighting for its life, he's grinning and all those lines and creases are in the right place again.

What? Mom says. What's the story here?

Him, Dad says. That little bugger.

We lean in from all around the table and look at the photo. It's one I passed by without even thinking about it. Allan in his swimming trunks, on a dock somewhere with three girls, none of which are his girlfriend. His arms are slung around two of the girls' necks, both of them blonde, and a third one with big tits and a bookish face is sitting on the dock, dangling her legs in the water, a towel on her head.

What's so funny about that? I ask, thinking it's something about hard nipples or a shrunken penis. And then I see it. One of the girls has her hand down the front of his shorts, and the other one has hers down the back. The one sitting down is looking up at him—they're all looking at him—and he's looking straight ahead, grinning.

Oh, jeez, Mom says and rolls her eyes. They're just friends, she says.

She takes the photo and I see the caption underneath the picture. It says *the gang*.

It's quiet for a minute and I'm not sure what's going to happen. We're all looking at Mom and Dad, going back and forth between the two of them, waiting for something to give. Then Marcus takes the photo.

She's sure got a hold of him, he says.

That's when all of us start to laugh, and we can't stop. Even as the machinery starts up again and our eggs and sausages and pancakes and coffee vibrate on the table. We're still laughing, even when ten consecutive blasts ring out like the end really is upon us.

165

THE EVICTION PROCESS

WE EVICT CHAMP first because we're worried he'll kill us. Even laid up in the hospital with one handset to rot off, he could do it. Even fucked up, bed-ridden and stuck in a room with another guy whose entire leg is swollen up like the Michelin man, he could do it. Champ has it in him. Look past his Huey Lewis hair, and you can see it in his face, all marked up like a tiger mauled him. He could go room to room and kill every patient, nurse, orderly, and doctor from here to the lobby if he wanted to. Jack's sixty-one, with a cane, and I'm not overweight but soft around the middle and weak everywhere else. We'd be nothing to him. This is why we've brought J.J. with us. He stands next to the bed, slapping himself, the only thing separating us from Champ. Before pulling us apart like Kleenex, he'd have to reach past the little boy he has so much affection for, or push him down, or step over him.

I have an entire quart of Iceberg in my pants, between my thigh and balls, and my concern is that if something happens, it might break, and I'll be drinking denim-filtered vodka until tonight.

When we closed the shop and didn't need someone like him around anymore, he said sure, like it was no big deal. Then went out and fought every man in some bar across the river. We heard about it on the news first, then someone said to me *that was the Champ you know,* and then I put it together. It could've just as easily been us.

We expect him not to take it well.

After we let him go, he had to take a job at the grocery store, this human pitbull forced to walk among college kids and goofy old moms, forced to unload cans of soup and detergent and whatever else. A load-picker. Didn't have enough money to go anywhere else, so we let him stay with us, and because he stayed, all the other guys stayed too, even though we weren't growing or selling or dealing or anything. And in the meantime, we'd been waiting for an opening. None of us has ever seen the Champ sick or hurt in any way—even after that big fight, he'd shown up with nothing more than a limp tacked onto his swagger and some cuts on his hands. Kept sticking his pinky in his ear like he had water in there but was otherwise unharmed.

It takes a miracle of international produce exchange—a brown recluse spider stowing away in a crate of oranges—for this to happen. One bite from this creature that isn't supposed to be here, a touch from this thing that shouldn't even be able to survive in our climate, and the Champ goes down. His hand is wrapped so thick it looks like a cartoon, a big white Goofy glove. Underneath, the flesh is necrotizing. And there are antigens flowing through his blood now, chemicals that no one knows. The story made it into the papers, too. The spider scientist they interviewed said it was a *near-impossible event.*

Jack gets right to the point. He says:

We're emptying the house.

We wait while Champ thinks it over. J.J. screams a couple times and I sort of squeeze him, but it doesn't do much. He whines, flaps his hands, and points at Champ's glove. But the Champ is all business. That body—with all of its strength and power, with all its years of taking beatings and dishing them out—doesn't swell up, doesn't flex, and doesn't turn against us. He gives Jack his good hand in a hearty clasp—the kind you might give to someone who just lost a family member.

Then he asks *when do you want me out*, and that's it.

For the first time that face, with all its pits and bumps and scars, makes him seem weak, or tired. They go over the details, share a more heartfelt round of handshakes, and it's over. No one kills anyone. Champ says he's enjoyed his time with us, and he even seems like he means it, too.

Then the guy with the diabetes leg, the man in the next bed blows everything. He's had enough and he says to us *control your fucking retarded kid*. J.J.'s been screaming since we got here, but we're all used to it and we hardly notice anymore. For us, J.J's wheezing, his clicks and grunts and moans, are on par with those soft, constant sounds that fill up the day—the hum of a washer and dryer, the hiss of wind through the yard.

One second Champ's in his bed, the next he's throwing open the curtain in his pineapple-print boxer shorts, his body all ribs and muscle like an Olympian. In the moments before anyone thinks to say anything, Champ already has the guy by his huge foot and he's wrenching it up, even using his big white mitten, too. Then he closes the curtain from the inside.

If Michelin Man says anything, he says it without enough bravery to break past a whisper. We only hear a few words, and they're all Champ's, in that quiet voice that scares the shit out of us:

kid

autistic

no

no

awful shame if

no

about manners

fucking leg

understand

no

polite

I would if I

that leg

no

ok then

fucking

mouth

clear?

Then Champ is back out, and that light is back in his face. Blood's pumping. There's even some shape inside those boxers. He gets back into bed and doesn't bother to close the curtain so the guy who almost got creamed is doing his best not to look at us.

Jack's face doesn't move behind his black glaucoma glasses because he's trying to act like what he just saw was no big deal. I know Jack is assuming it's a display of power. An intimidation tactic, and later he says exactly that. But I don't think it was at all. Champ puts his good hand on J.J.'s head while he talks and I can really see for the first time that he was never going to hurt *us*. The Champ would hurt the mailman or the guy behind the curtain or a guy who gives him grief at a bar, but never us. There's a flush of guilt that goes right through me, something I've felt a lot of for him, especially since he went from being a paid tough guy to a load-picker at the grocery store.

In the elevator going down, Jack says he thinks it went well because of painkillers, tapping his temple while he says it, but I know better. I nearly say what I've realized, which is *it went well because he's our friend, Jack*, but don't. I know Jack hates to be corrected, know that it isn't something he needs to hear, and know that I have nothing to gain by saying it. All I have is a fight to start. I think about the spot of blood on Champ's bandage, as if someone with too much lipstick had leaned over and kissed him there. Instead I say:

two down, three to go

Which is much more of a Jack thing to say, and he even gives me a little smile for it. We don't have anything else to say about it so I take out my bottle and have a nice, long drink while J.J. beeps and grunts in time with the elevator noises. I have an urge to run as soon as the door opens, cradle my vodka like a baby, and run up and out that ramp with the orange lights, run up to the surface and disappear. But I don't.

If the house weren't in such a shitty neighbourhood, the door would've been broken down long ago. It would've been broken down and me, Jack—all the deadbeats in our employ—we'd be in jail. J.J. would be taken from us, along with any and all assets related to the growth and cultivation of an illegal substance, and that would be the end of it.

Not anymore, mind you. Now, there's no drugs or hydroponic equipment to be found, and the only person

171

strung out on anything is me, or Morgan, who's using stuff with names like *BLOW OFF Keyboard Duster* and *Gorilla Glue*. When we pull in, we find him on the deck, lying on his back like a dead bug, his blond hair fanned out with dry leaves in it. Even with orange around his mouth and a paint-stained bag in his hand, he's as beautiful as ever. Breathtaking.

There was a time when Morgan used to fit right in, when he was a totally normal part of the scenery. Now the house is a *nice place*—has a fancy two-tiered living room with inlaid bookshelves and hyper-modern bathrooms, a stainless-steel macho kitchen with marble counters. We used to get drunk on the steps and throw our bottles and trash into the street like it was the eighteen hundreds. We used to have motorcycles parked in a row out front, with Odie's biker buddies buying vacuum-sealed bricks of weed the size of travel pillows. Morgan—with his cans of keyboard duster and spray paint and solvents—belongs to the old neighbourhood.

We'll get him later, Jack says.

We step over him, and go inside.

We used to watch the gentrification (what Champ called the *fancy-fication*)—the condos springing up, new businesses appearing, abandoned buildings getting pulled apart—and it scared us. One day, when we were having gin and tonics on the stoop, we saw a guy with a tie and a briefcase *on our street*. That was the scariest day of our lives.

Jack was a newspaper person once, and so he's aware of the correlation between a neighbourhood's income level and police presence. Always talked about it. If it became nicer, he explained, if there were happier, friendlier people—taxpayers, voters, citizens—it would be over. All the other telltale signs of a hothouse had been there: power bill through the roof, bars on all the windows, and the simple smell of skunky, earthy weed growing in plant pots by the dozen. But we knew that these things weren't enough to draw attention. People were needed for that. People who weren't zombies. People to complain and point fingers, wring their hands and say *that house* is a danger to the community. But we got out just in time.

Are you at least going to drink out of a glass? Jack asks me.

He motions to J.J., who is with his toys, and definitely *not* watching me, but who is at least nearby. I don't point out the obvious; if J.J. is capable of learning anything, it isn't going to be from any of us. We've had him for years and he's never copied us, never done anything remotely normal. His autism makes him like a person buried inside a pile of rocks. He can scream and writhe around—and not much else. It doesn't matter what we do around him. When I mentioned this before, I paid for it immediately. Had to go to the drugstore and find makeup the right colour and tint for the skin around my mouth. I also neglect to mention that Jack used to drink out of liquor bottles too; that was how we met. The news editor and a lowly carrier, both sneaking out to have cold sips of vodka in the alleyway near the breakroom.

Instead I say *oh yes sorry*, and hustle to the kitchen. I get a mug that says IF YOU'RE PUSHING 50, THAT'S EXERCISE ENOUGH, which doesn't at all match the new decor, though I certainly don't either. I fill it up, but my quart goes right back down my pants, where it safely wedges itself between my stomach and belt.

I think about the fight we could've had, if I had said no about the mug. With Jack, a yes or a no can take you anywhere—good or bad—so you have to choose carefully. I remember when the paper went under and Jack talked about an old piece of real estate he had, and the babysitting job he could give me. I had blown my internship and wasted my degree and was carrying papers instead of writing stories like I thought I'd be. I was thinking about jumping off the MacDonald Bridge. I remember exactly how I said yes to him, which was in a careful way—because I was excited, didn't want to mess it up, and wanted so badly to please him. I think about all the other men I could've said yes to, and what I would be instead.

I think about all that and watch J.J. slap his own face, watch Jack drink from my cup. I think about how everything is really just a bunch of yeses and noes, from cave people to your grandparents, all the way down to right now.

I know how this is going to go:

We're going to go through that steel door we put in (both to protect the product, and hold back the smell of it and its cultivators), except now that earthy, chemical smell is gone and it's replaced with something worse. We're going to smell the stench of B.O., cigarettes, and the black mould growing out of the drop ceiling, a smell like fish and feet and that pulpy hamster-cage odour that develops when no air circulates. It's going to be so thick we can pluck bits of it out of the airlike cotton candy. All of this will make Jack very upset.

There'll only be two of them down there, Odie and Will, and they'll be smoking and drinking and doing blow or meth or something I've never heard of. There was once carpet down there that has since been beaten down to a hard, black crust of spit and dirt and tobacco. Will's bare feet will be right on the stuff, in a spot that he's cleared of burger wrappers and broken glass, and little bits of crud. Will could be half-naked. Odie will be wearing the same clothes he's worn for weeks. That vest with a defunct motorcycle gang logo on the back. THE WANDERERS, with a bearded skeleton on a hill.

Will, who's old and feeble, will be affable and friendly. Odie, who thinks he's owed something from the world, will get shitty with Jack. And Jack will try to be cool, but inside he'll be boiling. He'll try out his *boss voice* and will make rational points: he's never charged them rent, he's given them lots of warning, and he's not being unfair by wanting to finish the basement. He'll be mad and I might have to pay for it.

Odie's face will turn to granite, his lower jaw will jut out, and his nostrils will flare like an early human. He'll say something, and then Jack will say something back, and from there, anything can happen. The big Bowie knife that Odie sometimes has on his belt might get plunged into Jack's chest. I can see a world where I jump in front and save him, and one where I don't. One where I watch him go down and do nothing about it, and one where I fall over his body and start screaming and crying. I can see a world where Jack puts the right words together and they go *sure thing, chief* and everything's like the good old days, when we were all pals; all the same kind of guys living in the same kind of place, all doing the same kinds of things. I can see a world where they get showered, put on clean clothes, and we have a last supper with all of them in the new dining room, at the new dining-room table, in the new dining-room chairs.

In all of these situations, Jack will come upstairs mad, either at the outcome, or the state of the place, or mad at the fact that he needs to change his clothes now. Or at me.

So when he says *come on, let's go down*, I make sure I'm sitting on the cream-coloured loveseat near the patio where J.J. likes to sit, shaking a stuffed animal at his dull face. Pretending to be enraptured with his son until he ignores me and goes down to complete the next eviction on his own.

When he was at the paper Jack believed—at all times—that there was a cabal out to get him, to dethrone him and install a new leader. In the alleyway, between our sips of vodka, he'd talk about it, and I would believe him, or convince myself that I did. So when he comes back upstairs, even though they were amenable and friendly, he's convinced there's something else going on. He looks through the living room, right past the spot where Champ and Odie once had a mercy fight and Champ popped two of Odie's fingers right out of their sockets and everyone was so fucked up we all started laughing and clapping like it was a stage play. He looks right through the walls like they aren't even here, his mind going wherever it goes when he's like this—to the past, or the future, or some place kept totally secret from me.

He's at the kitchen table in the exact spot where we used to drink and do lines and fuck around, his sock feet on a sun-warmed patch of hardwood—the spot where one of Odie's biker buddies threw up and no one noticed for weeks and weeks, until it hardened into the carpet like cooled lava.

If it's the past he's visiting, this could be precisely the vision he's having.

The next day they've opened the basement windows and begun chucking their shit out haphazardly. An old fan here, a card shuffler there. A busted-up lawn chair. Old clothes. It's building up slowly at the sides of the house, like it's purging them from its structure. I point this out to Jack in the best, most constructive way I can. It's happening. Champ has already been released from the hospital, has already come by and cleared out and scrubbed down the little room near the garage as soon as he could. He even took stains off the wall with a special sponge he lifted from the grocery store, invited us to have a look when he was done, hoping we'd be proud.

It's happening, I tell Jack. It's just happening slowly.

I'm holding J.J.'s hands at the wrist when I say it, so he won't hit himself. Jack has both hands on his shoulders, keeping him pressed into the kitchen chair while he works through this fit.

I know you're not a stupid person, Jack tells me, but you sure act fucking stupid sometimes.

I work hard to keep Jack out of the house, but then the only reason to go anywhere is the house itself—to buy new trim for the upstairs hall, paint, new pendant lights to hang over the new counters. When I try to come up with something else to do, he laughs at me— like I'm insane to want to go for a walk or to a movie or a bar. Whenever he's home, he's in the kitchen, staring at that black, metal door with his blacked-out glasses, thinking black thoughts.

I know I'm going to get it—it's just a matter of time until it comes my way.

One day, Jack catches Morgan sitting in the empty kiddie pool in the backyard, his head in a bag of some solvent or another. So he gets a baseball from the trash piles near the basement windows and whips him in the temple with it. J.J. and I watch this through the sliding doors. Other than the big red lump that grows slowly from his serene beauty, nothing is changed.

There's a long talk about what the next step should be. Jack's driven around looking for the Champ, checked out all his old haunts and bars, but he's not anywhere to be found. At the grocery store, they say he's quit, and we don't see him jogging in his too-short sweatsuit, those big hands sticking out from sleeves that stop at the middle of his arms. The idea is we can pay him to oust them, but he's nowhere to be found. I realize it was a fatal misstep to get rid of him first, but like every other thought I have, I can't safely express it to him.

The long talk takes us in and out of rooms, from the kitchen to the bedroom to the shower, where I sit and watch his vague shape behind the mottled-glass door. I drink from my mug and imagine him as a different man back there, and then I imagine myself as one. One who might go in there, bounce his head off the new tiles a half-dozen times, and be a man for once. A guy like the Champ, who might be able to take all this away from him, a guy who gets to say *no* at least some of the time.

The irony of taking Morgan to get help isn't lost on either of us. On our way to the addiction centre we stop at Wendy's, where I fill an empty cup with Iceberg. Jack and I share it for the rest of the drive, and a few times he even smiles at me for having brought it along. Using a straw makes it go faster, and soon everything is soft and light and easy to handle.

Jack and I had agreed once that being drunk in the daytime was like being on another planet. He said: *a planet almost exactly the same as this one, but a little better. A little more colour, a little more fun.* I liked that. That stuck with me.

The night before, he had said something like *tomorrow's our visit to the dog pound* and I got upset. Paced around, hid in the bathroom. Whisper-screamed shit to myself. Slept *downstairs-downstairs*, through the steel door and into the smell, where I shared the shredded couch with Morgan himself, who kissed my neck all night but was a soft nothing when I reached behind myself for his dick.

But today I'm leaning back to the seat behind me, and petting Morgan like he *is* a dog, careful to avoid the plum-coloured growth on his noggin. And I'm doing the same thing to J.J., too, so it's almost like we have two pets back there. Today, I've decided that Jack is right, and that I'm going to be good and do like he says from now on. Today, I feel more guilty than usual, and he's being nicer than usual. His eyes are hurting less today, I think, and on top of that, we're one step closer to the end.

Somehow, before we come to the stone walls and line of pine trees that surround the Addiction Centre, we lose Morgan. We lose him and end up driving in circles, taking the same off-ramp and looping around the same stretch of highway near a truckstop, over and over again. We hang our heads out the window to watch for him, and it's funny, because if Morgan were a dog like Jack said, this is exactly what we'd be doing if he'd jumped out a window. We'd be wringing our hands and shouting his name, watching for any sign of him, describing him to people at the gas station and leaving telephone numbers.

Eventually, we have to give up.

He's not our problem anymore, Jack says. What the fuck else can we do?

I don't look at him, do my best to agree, which I do by keeping my mouth shut and staring straight ahead for the hour-long drive home. It's the exact same thing I have to do when we get home and we can see that something's wrong even before we come to a full stop in the driveway. It looks like the door and windows are all open. But they're not.

All the windows are smashed. The walnut-panelled door is gone.

We find it in the living room, where it's come in through an obliterated side-window. The cream-coloured rug is smeared with shit, actual human shit, and I can see that it was smeared with actual human hands, too. Everything that can be smashed is smashed. Anything that couldn't be destroyed is covered in shit, or red paint, or both. There are holes in every wall, and all the wires are torn out, hanging like dead snakes from the ceiling and walls. The banister is completely ripped off the stairs and is now hanging out the back window. The stairs themselves are pulled up like finger-nails. The concrete counter where I used to make bread has been smashed haphazardly, like the surface of the moon. If I were to roll dough there now, it would come away with wild tumours from the craters and rise up in the oven like some deformed baby. The walls leading upstairs have a message for us—written with ball-peen hammer—dozens of black holes leftover from dozens of separate swings. We have to connect the dots:

F.A.G.G.O.T.S

J.J. is screaming, his voice rising and falling, the same sound over and over again like an ambulance.

If Morgan had stayed in the car, we would've been here to see it. We would've found them with hammers and buckets of paint and a crowbar, and maybe a chainsaw, from the looks of the couch. Maybe we would be in pieces, too. Maybe they would've cut me right in half and vodka would have gone everywhere. Maybe they'd have stomped on Jack's head so hard his eyes would've popped out of his skull and he'd finally have *ocular relief*. Maybe they would've taken J.J. and thrown him out the window rolled up inside the rug.

But Morgan did not stay in the car.

I made the mistake of asking him if he was ready to go, and he said *where*, and I said *to detox*, and that was it. He'd said no. Said it by opening the door and falling outside, rolling out of a moving vehicle going so fast we didn't even know he was gone. It was only when we took a turn off the highway and the door shut that we even realized it had been opened in the first place. As well as I can figure, he went into a ditch and through a drainpipe or something. Into another dimension, maybe.

When it's clear that we're not going to find him, and I start to cry, Jack tells me to stop. He says it immediately, at the first sign of tears, and says it with a hand cocked back, all ready to go, right into my mouth or my eye or the side of my skull. I try hard, but there's something that keeps catching, something about it that keeps on coming, so my chest heaves and hitches and I keep making little noises that make Jack's face red and furious. But I know he can't help it.

I think of the conspiracy Jack's already imagined, where I roll away from his innocent body and sneak into the night. Open that metal door and let those ghouls in one by one so we can plan his downfall at the kitchen table. I picture us as he must, as every kind of monster—a Dracula and a Frankenstein and a Wolfman and a Mummy and a Swamp Creature. I can feel how much he hates us, hates everyone that isn't himself. But I put those thoughts away.

Instead, when Jack looks at his house, covers his face and starts to cry, I go to him. I could hide somewhere, under the porch, or maybe in the rubble. I could run away, take the car and drive away, drive and go find Morgan and take the two of us to detox, but I don't. I have no choice but to go to Jack.

I know just what I'll need to say and do to get him through this. I'll tell him right away that we need to get out of here, that we should get a hotel and get drinks, relax and just not think about it right now. I'll tell him that this will all be better tomorrow and that insurance will take care of it. I'll tell him that the sun's gonna go down tonight but it's gonna come right back up tomorrow and the good stuff we got coming to us is gonna come—it's just gonna be a little bit late, that's all. In the meantime we got each other and we got J.J. and everything's going to work out, you'll see.

I put my arms around him and press his head to my chest, same as when J.J. has his fits, same as my father would do when something scared me, same as his father did with him, and so on, all the way back down the line to the very start of everything.

YOUR #1 KILLER

HE'S SMILING, BUT smiling too hard, like his teeth are going to shatter.

When he came out of baggage claim and rolled towards me with his luggage, I noticed it right away. He seemed frantic, and his eyes and head kept darting around like a lizard's. Even when we hug, I can feel him vibrating, his heart pounding and his temple throbbing against my head. He doesn't calm down in the car, either. He drums on the dash with his hands, fiddles with the vents. Opens the glove compartment and stares inside. We talk and he says he's missed me so much. He kisses my shoulder so hard I swerve a little. I imagine drugs in his luggage or bloodstream.

Then he reaches over and cranks up the radio, covers his mouth, and starts bawling his eyes out right next to me. He turns his head away (like if "You Can Go Your Own Way" is turned up loud enough, and he's looking out the window, I won't notice).

Chris, I say. Oh Chris.

Then and there I pull over on the highway and wrap him up in my arms. He balls himself up against me so small it's like he's turned back into a little boy again.

It feels like years ago, when an icicle fell off an over-pass and smashed against the windshield and cracked it down the middle on our way to Grandma's. His body hitching against me with the hum of the engine, his wet face on my neck. It feels exactly the same, but it's been eighteen years since I've held him and two years since I've even *seen* him so I'm not sure exactly what to do. I don't know what's wrong, why he's come back home, and he hasn't told me anything about it that isn't clearly a lie.

I take the safe bet and say the exact thing I did when the icicle almost killed us:

It's all right, and it's all over.

At home he does nothing, or at least nothing worth-while. He sits around a lot, usually on the carpet, or else upright in bed, watching TV or reading something or digging through old boxes of his stuff. It's either that, or he's in bed with all his clothes on, just staring. He claims that his girlfriend—a person I've never met—is dead and I can see that he's scared or embarrassed or regretful of whatever the truth of the situation is, so I don't press him, don't do anything that might set him off.

It's two months before he actually accomplishes something beyond looking out the window, eating cor-ner-store candy or diving for the phone when it rings. He digs out the Nintendo Entertainment System I bought him for Christmas in 1989, and he takes it apart and spreads it all over the living-room carpet to try to get it going. He wipes the stuff down, vacuums it, but it takes him a long time to put it all back together, and I have to step around the green electronics and chips and wires for days. After that, the sound of him sighing or coughing or smoking is replaced with the sound of skeletons and werewolves getting beaten to death by a beefy guy swinging around what looks like a boat rope.

I hear myself ask him:

Why don't you do something with your friends? I even add, pathetically, that maybe they could play a two-player game.

I don't have any friends, he says, making the little man jump around some steps.

He says it like I'm insane for suggesting it, like his friends have all died off, and I just haven't heard about it. For all that he's chosen to share with me, they could have.

So I don't say anything.

I leave him alone.

And I end up letting it go on for too long, mostly because I'm worried that if I say anything it'll be like the car again. I let him stay right there in the living room, a grown man surrounded by cups of juice and cereal bowls. I deliver takeout food to him, I clean up after and around him, around the spot where he kills giant bats and mummies and makes the basket of potpourri work overtime just to cover up his stink. Before I know it, he's been home for three months and we haven't spoken more than a handful of words to each other. He tries not to look at me and I try not to look at him, and the two of us do our best to pretend like there isn't something crazy going on.

When he was twelve, and he found out I was seeing a man, Chris stood on the kitchen table and demanded I bring him over. He swung a glass ketchup bottle around and said he wanted to give him *what for*. Shouted it like he was Yosemite Sam, his tiny eyeballs bulging out of his head, his crooked teeth flashing. He acted like he really meant it.

This time, if he's noticed I've had a man in the house for the past two years, he doesn't say anything. Nothing is brandished, not by anyone other than the little man in his video game.

I worked hard to wipe away any sign of Andrew: two whole days of cleaning to get everything squared away and how it was before. I got rid of extra food, the dog food, extra coat hangers, moved the TV back to the living room, gathered up and hid all of Andrew's shirts and shoes and *Economist* magazines. It's like I killed someone but forgot to hide the evidence for two straight years. Neighbours watched me with the boxes.

Then I told Andrew that we'd have to slow it down for a bit, which he didn't like at all. He's divorced after two decades of marriage, and I've been mostly single for just over ten years, so we are used to and expect different things from one another. We'll still see each other here and there, on dates or at his house, but this, he says, isn't enough.

I, on the other hand, feel fine about it. In the small rock garden in his backyard, Andrew tells me it's important that he meet my son, and that it isn't fair that I keep them apart. I tell him *life isn't fair*, which marks the first mom-ism I've used since Chris packed up his things and left years ago. After looking at an inukshuk he'd set up back there, and thinking about what I've said, Andrew tells me *we're all in this together*.

So I explain to him about the ketchup bottle and he scoffs. Says *hormones* like it explains everything. But he didn't see Chris's face that time and hasn't seen what it's been looking like these days.

I go about it the wrong way the first time around.

I decide if Chris gets a job it'll get him out of the house, get him doing things and saying things again. I don't really know what else to do, and when I talk about it, I can't really give him any incentives to go to work at Subway or KFC or Rogers, so he just looks at me with dead eyes when I bring it up. All I can say are wimpy things about doing something with himself and meeting people and making friends, obvious lies that mean nothing to either of us. Plus, I know from his bank statements that I can't even bring up money since his drug dealing or gambling or whatever scared him back home has left him pretty comfortable. He's labelled his online accounts, something I see people do at the bank every now and then—spouses divvying up accounts with their names, or with something they're working towards like **CUBA** or **COLLEGE** or **CAR LEASE**—but Chris's is something less ambitious:

SAVINGS	$18,961.22
SMOKES	$1,020.90

Why do anything if that's what your bank statement looks like?

The first time around I find a bunch of jobs and go get applications for him and they stay on the table next to his game cartridges and get shuffled under comic books and pizza boxes and motorcycle magazines in a matter of days. They sit nestled in his mess, and when I ask him about it, he makes up lies or excuses, anything to keep from doing what he needs to.

He doesn't have *his* computer anymore, so his resume is gone. And the word processor on the one in his room is fucked.

Fucked how?

It doesn't work. And the margins are all fucked up too.

So go to the library. Use the computers there.

That place is haunted, he says, which is the same thing he said about university when he dropped out two years ago. It's the way he talks about anything he doesn't want me to know about, including his ex-girl-friend, his last five or six jobs, and what's actually going on in his head. A joke and a lie mixed into one thing, shorthand for *fuck off, mom.* It's been like this since his first growth spurt put us eye to eye when he was fifteen and there was no one else taller to help out.

When he was eight and was asked to draw a picture of his family, he drew me and himself twice. Didn't even bother to change his size. When the teacher asked, Chris said it was because he didn't have a dad. *So I have to raise myself, basically.*

I have to wait for days and weeks for the next job-seeking step to happen, and when it does, it's a struggle for him to get his newly drafted resume on a disk. And then printed. And then attached to the applications. And then put in an envelope. A struggle to go get new applications because the old ones have pizza on them.

I get a pamphlet called *MENTAL HEALTH: You and Your Family* from my doctor. It talks about the importance of being able to differentiate between dangerous and normal behaviour before you decide to seek help for a family member. It tells us that it's both Mom and Dad's responsibility to watch for red flags—it even has a picture of a happy couple peering into a doorway together. It tells me to watch for other things too, like the big bottle of Extra Strength Tylenol in his room. It isn't exactly *right next to* the quart of rye that's been on his windowsill for the last five years, but it's close enough. And similar enough to the pamphlet's drawing of a bottle of beer, a joint, and a mirror of cocaine, that I feel a hot flash of panic standing in his room. Maybe this time it won't be like with the ketchup. Maybe he'll want to give himself *what for.*

In my lowest moment, I fill the applications out for him and send them out myself. When a guy from Staples calls and leaves a message and Chris doesn't bother to call him back, I slip back into an older version of myself. One that I thought was gone from me. I find myself standing over him, saying—shouting—the things I thought I could keep inside. Nothing that he needs to hear, and nothing he doesn't know.

It drives him back into his room, which at least gives me the opportunity to *really* clean the living room and pluck that grey Nintendo cartridge marked CASTLEVANIA from the machine and smash it with a hammer in the backyard.

When I ask him later, quietly, what this is all about, he just shakes his head. He's dissecting a fly or a spider with a pencil on his windowsill. Tells me to close the door. Once it's closed, he speaks a slow sentence and doesn't say anything more when I ask him to explain it. He says:

It's about different levels.

The phone rings in the middle of the night and he picks it up before I can even think about it. It's then that I cement what I already know: that she isn't dead, but

dead to him. Or more likely, it's *him* that's dead to *her*. In
a better place—and there with some other guy. I realize
it when he hangs up and I ask him who it was and he
says *nobody*. And then adds, after a minute of that long,
late-night silence, *fucking nobody*.

Andrew wants to help.

It's like when we first got together, him surprising
me at the bank with lunch, him bringing me movies and records I like, except he's always talking about
Chris. What to do with him, how he can help, what my
approach should be. His eyebrows rise and fall when
he's giving out advice, like he can't decide if what he's
saying makes sense or not.

He says that a job *is* the answer, but mentions other
things too. Says that Chris just needs to meet the right
girl, get something going with a pretty young thing.
Another time he says he just needs to do some hard
work and make some money. I think, but don't say, that
as far as I can tell these are the exact things that brought
him to where he is now.

It's about accomplishing something, Andrew says,
feeding treats to his fat brown dog.

He tells me *he* can talk to Chris if I want. He's never
had kids and I get the idea the talk wouldn't be so much
for Chris as for Andrew himself. I can feel all the ways
it could bother me, but there's something sweet in it,
too. I haven't filled him in on the whole story and don't
really want to, don't want him to know everything yet
and definitely don't want them to get together, so I kiss
his hand and tell him not to worry.

I tell him Chris has been doing odd jobs. It's a lie, of
course. He hasn't been out of the house except to buy

Colt 45 beer or lounge on the front steps and smoke. But just a couple days after I say he's been working it becomes true.

Mrs. Delong next door gets him to kill a skunk that's been waltzing around her property for days. I imagine she does this half because she actually needs his help and knows he has a rifle, and half because she wants to bring him over, have a look at him, and get the scoop on what's wrong with Ms. Rose's kid these days.

It seemed like a terrible idea to me, calling him instead of Animal Control when the thing is perched on a stump and acting nuts, but it does something for Chris. He smiles when he tells me it was spinning in circles in broad daylight, and actually laughs when he explains it was still spinning when he shot it.

It didn't even spray, he says.

I work hard to focus on the fact that he got up and put on clean pants and actually did something. Work hard to ignore the fact that he carried around the rifle for the rest of the day and focus on that smile, the big, goofy one he used to have; the one he first showed up with. Work hard—work very, very hard—to look past the skunk in the deep freeze, all wrapped in plastic. Ignore the other half of the skunk—the pelvis, legs, and tail, crudely sawed, or maybe chopped off with an axe—sitting in the trashcan beside the house and producing a smell so pungent it's like a hard blow to the stomach when I first open the lid. There was a book on the coffee table, *Home Taxidermy for Pleasure and Profit*, which appeared one day and disappeared the next. I try to justify the state of our skunk corpse with the presence of this book, but it isn't an easy thing to do.

I tell him I'm proud of him, but *proud* isn't the right word at all. It's more like less-worried-but-not-by-much.

Andrew decides he can't wait anymore and shows up after supper, unannounced, on my day off. Chris is on the step, smoking cigarettes and making a mean face. He's wearing clean clothes, but has his bathrobe over-top like a mental patient, big black sunglasses. Andrew is introducing himself, talking about himself, nodding and smiling way too much.

I immediately see all the specific, different ways this could go badly for each of them. I get terrified, furious.

But Chris is just ignoring him, his eyes on the street, smoking. He draws phlegm up his throat, spits, and watches it splatter.

When Andrew quits talking, I feel a fight sprout up between us that I know will carry on for weeks. I nearly tell Andrew it's over then and there, but I manage to keep it together, manage to keep my eyes on my son instead. Chris hacks and gurgles, spits, hacks some more. It's almost the same sound he'd make as a boy when his action figures would punch each other, or when he'd pretend something was being exploded.

When Andrew is gone, Chris starts a fire in the back-yard. It's the worst thing I've ever smelled—even worse than what was in the trash can—but he's standing right in front of the flames, still wearing those sunglasses even though it's night-time.

That was the skunk, he says.

It's here that I don't really have a hard time deciding if it's normal behaviour or not.

Just the lower half, he clarifies. We have to keep the top.

Chris helps another neighbour with a piano, gets it down her stairs and out of her house for her, and does it all on his own. Walks up there on his own accord, without any Post-It notes or snacks or encouragement. When I come home, he actually speaks up and tells me about it without me having to ask, the first time since Andrew's visit. I haven't seen much of Andrew, and except for short phone calls and a single visit to his house to get my jacket, we haven't spoken either.

It was her ex-husband's piano, Chris says, but she kept yelling at me like I was him. Like I left the thing there.

Did she pay you at least?

Yeah.

That's good, I tell him.

He draws something on the window (and wipes it away before I can figure out what). It's raining.

Do you like doing this kind of thing? I ask. Helping out and that?

People think they need people, he says.

He draws another picture on the kitchen window with his finger. A face with big eyes. It might be no one, but it might be her. Or maybe just the lady with the piano. Or me. Or Andrew, bright-eyed with his long hair, like in his college pictures. This time he doesn't wipe it away and the lines thicken on their own, bleed into fat shapes.

I ask him:

Maybe you could make a living out of this sort of thing?

He mutters something that ends with the word *alone* or *unknown*. I don't know which, and I don't care. I just nod and smile, and the next day I take out an ad in the *Guardian*, a listing in the yellow pages, and print cards up. I pick the name almost at random: EXTRA HANDS.

Do you need an extra set of hands? Help with odd jobs? Moving? Yard work? Chores? Call Chris at (902) 566-2880. He takes pride in helping others.

Andrew said odd jobs would be a good way to scare him back into school, that if you move enough fridges it puts your life into perspective fast. And he would've been right if all he did was dig up weeds and make lumber piles, but everyone wants him to use the skill set he'd displayed with Mrs. Delong. Everyone wants him to kill. He reads about killing bugs in his spare time, learns how to kill ants with hand soap, bees with a half-pint of mouthwash, and caterpillars with chili powder (though that'll kill most anything, Chris tells me).

He gets hired to kill rats, to shoot birds, to haul away an old carpet filled with silverfish and burn it. He does a lot of burning, on his customer's property or mine, and seems to get way too close to the flames once they get going, staring into it with those sunglasses on.

But he's talking again. Tells me about his jobs if he does things I'm not around for, and starts to get me involved when I am. Me with a bag on a stick, standing ready to catch the hornet's nest as big as a balloon while he saws it off a branch, dressed in a snowsuit with a snorkel and goggles on his head.

They only get you because of your breath, he says. So hold your breath when it comes down. Ever notice how they swarm your face?

No.

They swarm your face.

He cuts it down and it goes in the bag and I close it up and we're both laughing like crazy. The bag is alive with them, and there's a hum and a vibration like there's a power tool someone forgot to turn off in there.

Do you want to help burn them?

I decide then that this is maybe enough for me. After all, it *was* enough for a very long time. Maybe I don't need another grown-up to hold me and tell me he loves me. Maybe I just need to drive my son to old farmhouses and trailer parks and cook him dinners and just get by on that. Maybe I just need the few times he smiles and really means it—when his face lights up and you can see past his greasy hair and scrubby beard—and he looks like himself again. Maybe I don't need any of the things I thought I did.

I do it on the phone with the cord stretched all the way up the stairs and into my bedroom and Andrew tells me there's no need for any of this, that we can just take a break for a while if it's about Chris. And even though he sounds pathetic and condescending at the same time, I can feel our two years together really pushing against me, so I tell him quietly: *okay.*

Chris stops talking to me again. He still goes out and does jobs, but walks to them or else takes the bus. When I ask if he needs a lift he says no, and when I ask him *what did I do* he shrugs or says nothing, walks away. I imagine it's the same mental process as looking at the phone and not answering when I would call him before he moved back. The same thing as staring at the receiver or reading at my name on Caller ID and doing nothing about it. Same as throwing out the birthday cards that I mailed to what everyone told me was the worst neighbourhood in Montreal.

He takes to staying out really late, then sneaking back inside to sleep for a few hours only to slip out again before I get up for work. The signs that he'd even set foot in the house are small; more of those jumbo beers come or gone from the fridge, or a soaked patch of mud and grime by the hose where he sprayed his work boots off.

Money begins to appear on the coffee table where his magazines and pizza used to be. Seven hundred and fifty dollars, a sum he must've decided was fair for rent and food and putting up with this bullshit.

I find him one night while driving around, acting like I'm *not* looking for him. He's at the ballpark near the house, shooting his bow and arrow, firing it straight up into the air. I honk and flash my lights, but he doesn't get in.

What are you doing? I shout.

I'm killing bats, he says.

And then I can see them, up in the air near a patch of moon, flapping in a crazy cloud. I watch his arrow sail into them and keep going.

Is someone paying you?

No.

Do you want a thermos?

I have two. His old Garfield one, filled with beer. And the new one, filled with coffee.

No, he says. I'm fine.

It's the most he's said to me in maybe two weeks and the first time in two weeks I get to see him for an extended period of time. So I stay and drink the rancid beer out of that orange cup and watch. He gets three, then lets me take him home. He's driven his bats onto one arrow like a shish kebab. He keeps whirling it around in his hands. Their dead wings clap for us, or maybe just for him.

Eventually I end up at Andrew's. He gets me off twice and says after that he's missed me, and that he's sorry. I say *for what* and he just looks at me, sweating and breathing heavy. I kiss him, and press myself against him. Look up at his face and try to see if I'm right or wrong—if it feels good to be with him or if it just feels good to *not be alone.*

Later, he drives me home, and I let him come inside. We still have our coats on when the two of us listen to a message on the machine from Grodd River Golf Course. They say that something's wrong with Chris, that I should call them as soon as possible.

Right away Andrew speaks: I'm coming with you.

Holding my arm: You can't expect me to not care about your child.

And then, arms at his sides, his head low: I care about you.

I don't respond to any of it because I can't. I wait with the door open for him to leave. Then I go there on my own, everything fast and blurry and running together like the pace of things in a dream. I can see what's coming—know just what it's going be like, the position his body will be in—and exactly what I'll do when I see it.

At the golf course, the guy drives me across the green and tells me what happened—how Chris went out to set up traps for their gophers after they were closed and didn't come back. He explains that he had to go find Chris before he could lock up, and found him lying on the ground. And he wouldn't get into the cart. Chris said he was listening for gophers and refused to get up or do anything the guy asked him to.

Just laying there. Who does that?

I don't know, I tell him.

He keeps saying it—*who does that*—like it's just some wacky, inconsiderate thing Chris is doing for a laugh. The cart has no lights, so he's given me a giant flashlight to guide us through the dark, but I don't know where we're going and have trouble keeping the white beam straight and steady. When we're between the lit patches of golf course, the grass looks like desert, and the sand traps look like lakes. The actual lakes look like tar, like something that could swallow up a body and keep it intact for thousands of years.

I'm expecting Chris to be catatonic or screaming or just plain crazy. Or motionless with a belly full of pills, or half his head missing. I expect there to be something so big and life-changing and horrible waiting for me that I almost want to get out and just lie down myself. I feel a weakness in my arms and legs, my throat beginning to close over like a poisoned insect.

At the eighteenth hole, I'm only half inside my body.

But when I shine my light across the hills, across the water hazard and down the final slope, he isn't there. We pull up to where he's supposed to be, and there's just a messy square-ish hole right there in the green, with cigarette butts all around it, and a perfect square of green grass and earth next to it. And three brown lumps.

Groundhogs, all in a row.

They're dead, and I can't immediately see how. When I shine the beam on them, there appears to be no blood whatsoever, like he was just able to somehow stop their hearts from beating.

Oh, the golf course guy says. He got them.

He did, I say.

He moves one of them with his foot.

I thought he was just fucking around, he says.

I nearly tell him *me too*.

He drives me back to the gate, and even though I know Andrew's going to be waiting for me in the parking lot, I watch the treeline. I try to imagine what it must be like to walk out there, through the forest, onto the road and down the highway. To walk forward and into a place you don't know, by yourself, and make your way across all that distance, in the dark.

He's home when I get there, up in his room.

I don't know the last time I saw inside, but he's left the door open, so I go in. It's dark, but I can tell it's different. There are no more comic books or pizza boxes, no more bowls of cereal stacked in stinking towers. He put down a rug, and there's a bookshelf and a filing cabinet that wasn't there before. There's a table pushed against a wall with electronics on it. Printers or scanners or a fax machine, their buttons glowing green and red. Another dull lemon glow coming from an outlet. An air freshener. Things have been moved into place while I wasn't looking.

He's at his desk, his lenses lit up by his computer screen. I watch him flip through pictures of ants and gas canisters, going back and forth between them and some kind of flyer or newsletter. Watch him paste a dead mouse onto an empty field, give it a thick red outline with another click.

You break up with that guy, he asks.

Probably because he's been (and still is) smoking, his voice is rough and dry, like an old man's.

Yes I did, I tell him.

Because of me.

Yes.

That's stupid, he says. Then he flips between some windows and brings up a yellow box with green letters. Tells me to look at it.

It reads:

YOUR #1 KILLER
of pests and small animals
CALL
'REMORSELESS' CHRIS ROSE
(902) 566-2980

I changed the company name, he said.

I see that.

I'm gonna stick this guy in that blank space here. He flips to another window and shows me the mouse again, magnifies its face so I can see the tiniest pricks of blood coming out of its nose and mouth, its eyes bulging out of their sockets.

Great.

You shouldn't break up with some guy just because of me, he says. He turns his cursor into a black brush and makes the droplets disappear, one by one.

Then he turns around.

His hair is getting long and curly and his beard has absorbed all the missing patches so that his face is one big scribble—his smooth cheekbones and wide lips hidden away.

You deserve to be with somebody.

And what about you? I ask. And I expect one of *his* answers. One of those half-jokes that burns right through me.

We're talking about you, he says.

He's wearing his heavy work coat over a spring jacket over a hooded sweatshirt, layers and layers separating him from me and everyone else, with just the tiniest bit of skin peeking out.

The phone rings just then—down in the living room—and he doesn't move, doesn't get up. Instead, he puts the cursor on the mouse's grey face, where it turns into a little white hand, and then a fist. He drags the picture over to the words, and places it exactly where it belongs. Then he taps the screen, right between the creature's eyes. The phone keeps ringing and ringing.

I took this picture, hey? It's one of mine.

Good stuff, I tell him. Good.

Acknowledgements

I WROTE THE first of the stories collected here when I was 23 and completed the last one at age 30. They might be the only things I have ever taken seriously in my life, and have been challenging enough that I've had to reach out for help many, many times. This page is necessary to thank all the gifted, gracious people who I have asked so much of, and who gave me their very best without asking anything in return.

I dedicated this book to Alexander MacLeod and Ryan Paterson for the work they've put into these stories, and for supporting this project from the start. Alexander took a chance on me, was patient with me, and believed in me. Ryan has always pushed me to be better. Without these two, there would be no *Bad Things Happen* (and maybe no Kris Bertin either).

A big thanks to my fellow students from the Saint Mary's creative writing workshop (especially K. Murray) who helped me find my voice and get my first work published. Thanks to the magazines who printed me: *The Antigonish Review, Words & Images, The Malahat Review, Riddle Fence, Joyland, TNQ, PRISM International, and EXILE.* Thanks to Nick Mount at *The Walrus,*

Lee Sheppard at *Pilot Pocket Book*, Mark Jarman at *Fiddlehead,* and Ben from *ResumeQuest* for all their extra help. Thanks to Amy, Dave Richards, and Mike Christie, who said (under duress) some very nice things about me and this book. Thanks most of all to Dan Wells and the people at Biblioasis for their dedication and extraordinary effort in making this book a reality.

Thanks to my normal friends, and to my friends who are writers. Thanks to my family, especially Jeremy & Patricia, who put me up so I could work on this stuff more than once. Thanks also to my other family at Bearly's—staff and customers both—who have always encouraged me, bought my stories, or supplied the raw materials with which to make them. I love you all, but I love you the very most, Ashley.

Finally, I wish to apologize to all the friends, family members, girlfriends, coworkers, employers, customers, pets, and professors whom I have continually disappointed and neglected in order to write these stories.

I'm sorry, but I couldn't help it.

KRIS

ABOUT THE AUTHOR

KRIS BERTIN IS a writer from Lincoln, New Brunswick. He bartends in Halifax, Nova Scotia.